BOOK ONE

PROTECT *me*

USA TODAY BESTSELLING AUTHORS

J.L. BECK & C. HALLMAN

Editing by: Word Nerd Editing

Cover Design by: C. Hallman

1

eira

I STARE at my brother's lifeless body on the floor of my apartment. I know what I need to do next, but I can't move. My feet remain cemented to the floor, my brown eyes moving over the scene before me. There is blood...so much blood.

I bite into my bottom lip hard—hard enough to draw my own blood. I won't scream. I can't. Leo told me if someone ever came for him, I was to go to a man, one of his friends, and he would protect me, but I can't remember his name.

My stomach rolls, bile rising into my throat. I place a hand over my mouth to stop the impending vomit.

My brother is dead.

My chest tightens; my hands fist at my sides. My brother is dead. Actually dead. We joked about this moment many, many times, but looking down at his lifeless body, his vacant stare, I know this isn't a joke.

Start moving, a little voice inside my head says.

I look at the message the bastards left on my fridge. The sticky note shakes in my hands as I read the words over and over.

I'll be back for you.

I shiver involuntarily. I need to find the man my brother wanted me to go to. I have a feeling he's the only one who can protect me now.

With unsteady hands, I pull my phone out and go to my emergency information. I created a small doc simply for this very thing. Leo had only given me a name and address, saying it would be enough.

But how can I show up on someone's doorstep with this kind of thing? Leo said the person would understand—they'd know why I was there—but I didn't believe that...not one bit. Too afraid to go into my bedroom or even stand inside the kitchen another minute, I walk out the door, closing it quietly behind me.

Tears fall from my eyes, staining my cheeks. I have never felt so much pain and confusion all at once. My lungs seem to deflate, refusing to fill no matter how many breaths I take.

I make it two steps down the stairs when I hear voices coming from the level below me. I spot two guys talking, both with accents—Russian maybe. I'm not concerned until the words meet my ears.

"The boss said he wants the sister for himself, so don't fuck her up too bad." The men are big and burly, way bigger than me, and definitely stronger. If they get their hands on me, I'm as good as gone.

Move, Kiera! My brother's voice fills my head as I try to stop the tensing of my muscles. I have to get out of here. If they catch me...I shove the thought away before it takes root.

As soft as my feet allow, I tiptoe backward, away from the staircase. I slip my shoes off and start walking up the stairs in my socks. Staying close to the outside, I make sure they can't see me if they decide to look up through the middle of the stairs.

With my lip caught between my teeth, I hold in the scream that wants to rip from my throat. Fear consumes me, my muscles remain rigid, but I continue onward. I walk all the way to the top floor and take the emergency stairwell down.

I'll be safe, hidden from their gazes—a secret passing through. My entire body shakes as I take the steps two at a time, my eyes passing over my shoulder every few seconds, causing me to trip. Landing against the railing, it digs into my ribs. I need to pay better attention or I'm going to get caught.

I sigh in relief when I make it down the stairs. I am only in my first year of college. I'm supposed to be partying, hanging out with other people my age, not discovering my dead brother's body, or running away from two monsters who want to drag me back to their boss. The image of being attacked by one of them flickers in my mind.

No. I will myself to calm down. I'm right there, hanging on the very edge of losing control. I want to cry, scream, yell, but I know none of those things will happen. Pushing through the back doors of the apartment complex, I run down the street, my backpack still resting heavily against my back.

I sprint down the street and hide behind a group of trees before I decide to stop and catch my breath. My little legs do nothing to help me when it comes to running. I pull out my cell phone and enter the address into the map.

A little icon pops up on the screen, confirming it works. I sag against the tree, waiting for it to load.

Would they track my phone? Who are they to my brother? Dozens of questions rattle off inside my head. I didn't even say goodbye to him. My gaze drops down to my phone. The map finally loaded.

Fear pumps through my veins. Hopefully, whoever I'm going to see will know more than I do. Otherwise, I'm screwed.

The idea of being caught by those sinister men makes me move faster. My map pinpoints the location to somewhere called Night Shift.

After walking for what seems like forever, I arrive at the building, my eyes gliding over it. I clench my jaw in anger.

It's a strip club.

There's a sign plastered to the front window.

NOW HIRING: BEST STRIPPERS IN THE AREA.

My mouth goes dry. Why did my brother send me to a strip club? This has be some kind of sick joke...a chance for him to get back at me after death? Shivering, I grow afraid of the idea of going inside. Who am I asking for, and what if they tell me to leave? I wrap my arms around myself as a cold breeze blows through me.

Go inside, the same voice from earlier demands. I know I'm slightly unhinged, even more so because I'm hearing things inside my head, but it's my body's warning—my body's way of making me do something I don't want to because I'm too scared.

Dragging my feet across the concrete, I grip the metal door, the cold of it making all the warmth inside me dissipate.

I open the first door, and then a second, my feet moving on their own. I'm shaking like a damn leaf in the wind. I want to rewind time and go back to this morning when my brother was alive and joking with me.

When my feet stop moving, I realize I am at the bar. The inside isn't as bad as I thought it would be. There is a huge stage with a large seating area centered around it on the far side of the room, and a long hallway off to the left.

"If you're looking for the boss, he's in his office."

I lick my lips nervously, swallowing some of the fear down.

"Which way?" I barely get the words out. The women in front of me eyes me curiously, her hazel eyes piercing mine. She looks to be ten years older than me, her face all dolled up with makeup. Her curvy body with hardly any clothing on it. Her breasts all but falling out of her top, and the shirt—if you could even call it one—only covers half her stomach.

If she wore a bathing suit, it would have covered more skin.

"Down the hall that way." She hooks a thumb in the direction of the hallway off to the left. "Follow it until the very end and turn left. You'll see a big man standing outside his office, that's how you'll know you made it." The mystery woman smiles warmly.

My legs quiver as I head off, fear of the unknown slithering up my spine. I don't know what I'm walking into. From the looks of the place, women are nothing more than objects, and I don't want to be an object, not for anyone. I don't even want to be looked at, let alone touched.

Again, I question why my brother sent me here.

Walking down the dimly lit hall, I pass numerous wooden doors. A couple moans and screams have me scurrying faster, my feet slipping all over the floor. When I make it to the end of the hall, I turn left and stop. There's a door directly in front of me, but no man standing outside it.

Am I in the right spot?

I trace the engraved letters on the door.

DAMON ROSSI.

I blink slowly. Below his name is one single word:

BOSS.

My stomach churns, and I press my hand against the door more firmly to hold myself up. I'm going to pass out. I know it. Today has pushed me beyond my limits. I'm scared out of my mind and have nowhere else to go. I guess I could go back home and be killed—or worse, caught by those bastards. Or...I could get my shit together, walk inside the office, and find out who Damon Rossi is to my brother. Taking a calming breath, I grab the brass knob and turn it slowly, then hold my breath as I push the door open. A low creaking sound emits from the damn thing. I exhale a moment later and poke my head inside.

I can't help but feel like a rabbit caught in a snare. Like something bad is about to happen.

My heart is racing, and my palms are sweaty. It's like I'm an intruder, but I force myself to stay put. My brother wouldn't have sent me here if he didn't think I'd be safe, right? The fact that I need to find out who Damon is pushes me onward. I let my backpack slide off my shoulder, and deposit it onto the chair in front of the desk.

My fingers trail against the mahogany wood, and I walk around the room. There's a manliness about this place.

It's dark and sinister, and smells of tobacco and whiskey. Files lay on his desk with girls' names written on the front of each folder. I open one out of pure curiosity, and gasp, closing it quickly when I see the picture of a naked woman in a very provocative position.

My gaze drops to a drawer under the desk. I know I shouldn't be snooping, and I don't really know what I'm looking for, but I feel the need to search...for something...anything. I reach for the handle, but when I try to pull it open, I realize it's locked.

Looking around the room in disappointment, I realize there's nothing else for me to find in here. Walking back around the desk, I'm about to sit down on the couch when I feel the air shift around me.

A warmth fills the air...light mixed with dark.

My heart beats a million miles per minute, and the hair on the back my neck stands up. I've escaped one monster only to be trapped by another.

I'm frozen, too terrified to move, when I hear someone behind me. I suck in a sharp breath. It hurts my lungs, but helps build the shrill scream about to leave my throat. I feel hands on me, and they're those of a man. The roughness of his touch is unforgiving—as if he's angry and wants to punish me.

Before my scream can make an appearance, I'm pushed face-first onto the couch. I'm in full-on panic mode now. I try to get up, but he leans his large body into mine, making it impossible for me to move. His grip is relentless, and when I feel something hard pressing against my ass, I gasp.

No. No. No.

"Usually, I don't fuck women in here, but since you seem so interested in my office, I suppose I should give you the grand tour while you ride my cock."

My eyes squeeze shut, and my body freezes. My brother sent me to be raped. Tears prick my eyes. My yoga pants are ripped down my legs, and I start to shake while sinking deeper into the cushion. I want the moment to be over. I bite the inside of my cheeks. The copper taste of blood fills my mouth, and I focus on the bitterness of it.

"If you want the job you, can't be so tense. No one wants to fuck a piece of board," a dark voice whispers against my hair.

A shudder runs through my entire body. I'm not sure I'll ever get his deep, gravely voice out of my head again...

amon

Why the fuck is this bitch so tense?

I can't have a girl work at my strip club if she is going to be this uptight. Her back isn't even bowed, and she looks uncomfortable as fuck. Still, it would be a shame to send this one away.

Maybe she's playing hard to get. I smirk. I love it when they play hard to get. The rougher the better.

I reach for the waistband of her stretchy yoga pants and pull them down roughly. She whimpers underneath me, and again, I wonder if it's an act. It has to be an act. No one shows up here, especially a woman, without expecting to get fucked. I rub my rock-hard cock between her ass cheeks, making it crystal clear what I want.

She's got a nice body, a plump ass, and enough meat on her hips for me to grip onto when I pound into her.

"You know, for someone who snuck into my office and waited for me...you play really fucking hard to get. Is this how you like it?" I lace my fingers into her hair and nip at her ear, growling the words. I'm getting seriously fucking frustrated.

I reach around her body and slip a hand into the front of her panties. Expecting to find her cunt wet and ready, I'm surprised when I find her soft, warm clit dry. She isn't here to fuck me. Fucking pity. Hopefully, I don't have to kill her.

I pull my hand away from her pussy and loosen my grip on her hair, but I don't release her yet. She's not going to get away from me that easily.

"Who the fuck are you?" I growl, my fingers slipping to the back of my jeans, resting against my gun. If she is not here for the job or to get fucked, then what the hell does she want?

"M-M-My brother...sent me." She stumbles over her own words, and my gaze rakes over her body. Her bare ass is shaking...her entire body...

"He's dead..."

I flip her over onto her back so I can see her face.

She doesn't look familiar, and I would definitely remember a pretty face like hers. Beautiful brown eyes almost too large for her heart-shaped face, and those lips...they're plump, fuckable. I want them around my cock—preferably right now—but I doubt that's going to happen tonight.

She looks at me with fear in her eyes, her body trembling. It bothers me, but not enough for me to stop myself from pulling my gun out. I'm not fond of killing women, but I do what needs to be done.

"Who the fuck is your brother?" I snarl. My body is still impossibly close to hers. If she tries to escape, I'll have my hand wrapped around her throat in a second.

I watch her face. Her lips quiver. There is no way she is the sister of one of my men. No one who is affiliated with us gets this terrified over a simple question. But then again, I've seen grown ass men piss their pants dealing with me.

"Are you fucking deaf?" I press the barrel of the gun into her side, right between her ribs. If I pull the trigger, she'll die. There's no way around it.

"Puh...puh...please don't." Tears stain her cheeks.

I lean closer, smelling her fear, but beneath it, I get a whiff of strawberry. It's faint, barely there, but it makes my mouth water. I suddenly have the ridiculous urge to kiss her.

What the fuck?

I don't kiss. I don't cuddle. I don't do dates. I don't do shit that could possibly lead to anyone thinking I like a girl for anything other than the hole between her legs.

But this girl...she has me intrigued. She's different from the girls I usually have at my mercy.

She also still hasn't told me who her fucking brother is, and that's pissing me the hell off. I ask a question, I get a fucking answer.

"I'm not used to asking twice so you better give me a fucking answer now before I blow your brains all over my office."

"Le...Le...Leo is...w-w-was my brother. He...he's dead."

Fuck! Fuck! Fuck!

Leo told me about his little sister a while back. I don't know much about her, but I do know she knows nothing about the shit her brother was caught up in. He asked me watch out for her incase something bad happened. And promising to watch out for her was the only way I could get him to do some of the more risky drops. I didn't think that promise would actually show up in my office one day.

What the fuck am I supposed to do with her? She is not my responsibility. So what if I told him I'd look after her. It's not like her brother is going to come back to life to see if I kept my promise.

I move toward my desk. Sinking into the leather chair, I prop my feet up on the edge, and order, "Pull your pants back up." I can't have a half-naked girl in my office and not fuck her. I'm already going to have blue balls as it is. Maybe I'll take that new stripper for a test ride...what's her name? Amanda? Anna?

My attention shifts back to the present. Kiera...or Kilie, I think is her name. She sits very still for a long moment, and I worry maybe she didn't hear me. She's not gonna last one fucking day here if she doesn't learn to do as she's told when she's told.

I bite my tongue, stopping myself from saying anything else. It's not something I do often, and I'm not really sure why I do it for her. The girl finally scurries to get her pants back on, then grabs her backpack off the chair and heads for the door.

I almost snap. God, she's a pain in the ass.

"I don't remember saying you could leave." She stops dead in her tracks, and I smirk. It's fun to know I have some type of control over her.

"Sit your ass back down. We're done when I say we're done." I can see her legs shake from across the room, and wouldn't be surprised if they gave out, sending her plump ass to the floor.

She wears her emotions on her face. She's weak. Filled to the brim with fear—and over what? I've watched many of my men die, have killed people who didn't really deserve it, and I never felt a single drop of remorse.

So why the fuck am I feeling sorry for her?

"How do you know he's dead?" My gaze turns to slits.

"I found him," she says, her voice shaky. Her brown eyes refuse to meet mine, and that's infuriating. A person's eyes are the portal to their soul. How can I be sure she is telling me the truth if she refuses to look me in the eye?

"I found him in my apartment," she finishes, visibly swallowing.

"Did you call the cops?" I ask, and this time when she looks at me, her brown eyes go wide and she shakes her head. At least she wasn't dumb enough to phone them. "Write your address down." I throw her a pen and piece of paper and watch her scribble something down. When she's done, she gets up to hand me the items, but her hands are so damn shaky, she drops the pen.

She gets down on her hands and knees beside my desk, searching for it. As if my cock wasn't pressing uncomfortably against my zipper already.

Fuck this girl.

A second later, her head pops up and she places both the items in front of me, before pushing up from the floor. I'd love to see the look on her face when I tell her how much blood has been spilt on this floor.

"Why...why do you need my address?"

"Well, I need to send a cleanup crew out for one, and two I've got to figure out what the hell kind of shit your brother was into to get him killed." She winces at the mention of her brother, but I don't have the time or patience to tiptoe around her feelings. "Do you have a phone?"

"Y-yes."

"Give it to me."

She digs in her girly backpack and hands me the phone. I smash it on the floor, then step on it for good measure. I can't have her calling people or taking pictures from inside my office. She stares up at me, but doesn't say anything. Thank. Fucking. God.

"Stay here, don't move, and don't fucking touch anything."

Getting up, my chair scoots back on the hardwood floor. Even that simple noise makes her flinch. Jesus, what the fuck is wrong with her? Was she abused? Attacked?

I think back to the way I treated her a few minutes ago. Guilt pricks my conscience. Fuck me. At least she's not like all the other women who only want to throw themselves at me.

Shaking my head, I make my way out of the room, closing the door behind me. I pull my key out of my pocket and lock the door.

Now that she's here, she's a liability. A loose end. And I can't risk having her fuck up my entire life because she doesn't understand how dark and dangerous world this is.

I find Toni in one of the back rooms and give him the address on the paper.

"Send a cleanup crew out there right now. If anyone gives you trouble, contact Shane."

"Sure thing, boss." He takes the paper and gets up from the leather couch. There we go—how it's supposed to be. I make an order and shit gets done. No questions asked, no comments, or whimpering. Now, I need to figure out how I get the chick in my office to do the same.

I rub my jaw. It has been a while since Leo did work for me. I'd have to wait for the cleanup crew to get back to see who's possibly responsible for this shit. Every gang has their own way of killing people. Some carry it out over hours, torturing, cutting, and destroying. Others simply place a gun to someone's head and pull the trigger. From the look on Kiera's face, I'm assuming it wasn't a bullet wound her brother died from.

Jesus, I need a drink...and a blowjob.

Fuck babysitting.

I'm not keeping that girl.

No. Fucking. way.

iera

DID he lock me in here?

I can't get my stupid hands to stop shaking, or the rest of my body, for that matter. I don't want to be here—in this room...or anywhere near Damon Rossi. I should've known coming here was a bad idea. Why the fuck would Leo send me to this guy? Better yet, what the hell had my brother been doing to get himself killed?

I ponder the thought for a long time, standing there, not wanting to sit. My eyes move to the wooden door holding me inside this room.

Even though I know he locked the door when he left, I still walk over to it and check. My fingers close around the cool brass knob. When I try to turn it, it's no surprise that it's locked.

I walk back to where I was standing before, my gaze moving to the couch. The couch where he pinned me down...

Shivers rack my body. I felt violated, terrified, but even so, the feeling of his hands on me was intoxicating—something I never want again.

I have no idea how long I've been in this room, but it feels like forever. Judging by the loud music and chatter outside the office door, the club must be open now. I consider banging on the door and yelling for help, but something tells me the people who come here and work for Damon wouldn't do a damn thing to help me. If anything, they'd help him.

The longer I sit inside this room all alone, the more terrified of the unknown I become. When is he going to come back? What's going to happen to me? Will he kill me? I remember the look in his brown eyes as he pressed the gun to my ribcage. There was no remorse...no kindness. My thoughts continue to run rampant, upping my anxiety. A key rattling and the sound of the door being unlocked drags me out of the abyss, and I stand.

The door opens slowly, and the same lady from this morning sticks her head into the room. "Hey, sunshine, you hungry?"

Starving, actually. I haven't eaten all day. "I could eat something."

I watch her wearily. The door opens farther, and she walks in holding a plate with a variety of food on it.

"Thank you," I tell her when she hands it to me, as well as a bottle of Coke she has under her arm. She nods and turns on her heels to leave.

"Hey, can I ask you something?" I keep my voice calm. I have no reason to be afraid of her, right?

Looking back over her shoulder, her eyebrows raise. "Depends on what kind of question you're asking."

I nibble on my bottom lip for a moment. "What kind of work do people do around here for Damon?"

I don't think Damon would tell me what my brother did for him even if I could muster up the courage to actually ask him. This might be the only shot I have at finding an answer.

"Most of the girls just strip, but some do more for extra cash."

"Oh...What about the guys he has working for him?" Her eyebrows suddenly draw together, like my question angers her.

"Don't ask shit like that around here. That will only get you in trouble. If you want to know about working here as a stripper or hooker, I'll fill you in with all the info you'll ever need before taking the job. Other than that, don't ask questions you don't want answers to."

Her words chill me to the bone.

Don't ask questions you don't want answers to.

"Sorry," I mutter. Clearly, I'm barking up the wrong tree with some of my questions, but I am curious to know more about the women who work here.

"Why do girls work here?" I don't understand how anyone would work in a place like this...for a man like Damon.

She shrugs. "The money is good, and Damon lets the girls keep a fair amount of what they make. He also doesn't pimp them out unless they want to be pimped out."

There is a moment of silence that settles between us, and then she continues. "He doesn't force any of them into prostitution. That's better treatment than you'll get from any of the other clubs around here."

I nod like I understand, but I don't. I don't understand any of it. How could a woman sell herself to a man—to be used...for pleasure?

If the way Damon treated me earlier on the couch is an example of the way his men treat women, then I want to get the hell out of here as soon as possible.

"It's okay. You don't have to work here if you don't want to. Damon won't force you into something you don't want."

Uneasiness filters into my veins. Obviously she doesn't know the Damon who showed himself to me a few hours ago. If she did, she'd probably think differently...or maybe she wouldn't because she's so used to this behavior.

"No offense, but I don't want to work here. I don't want to be touched, or even looked at. This place and these people terrify me."

She nods and smiles. Her expression makes me feel warm inside.

"No offense taken, honey. Eat your food, relax, and I'll be back later to see if you need anything, okay?"

I nod, my eyes going to the plate in my hands. The woman turns around and walks out of the room, closing the door softly behind her.

I listen for the lock to be turned back into place. When I don't hear anything, I scurry across the floor, my heart beating loudly in my ears.

Can I really escape? I'm not sure where I'll go, or even what I'll do. With my brother gone, I have nowhere to live, and no way to pay my bills. That's not even mentioning the men who are searching for me—the ones who left that scary ass note on my fridge. I forgot to tell Damon about the note and the men I saw in the stairwell at my apartment.

Would it really matter if I told him?

A part of me says no. He's heartless, dangerous, and oozes arrogance. I'm naive...I know this. My brother reminded me often, but even I'm not dumb enough to get mixed up with Damon.

I want to run—no, I'm pretty sure I need to run. The fear of what may happen to me if I stay controls my movements. In Damon's presence, I am weak and afraid. All of this—these people and this place—leaves me scared.

I can't stay.

I won't.

After waiting a few more minutes to make sure she has walked away, I open the door enough to stick my head out. When I don't see or hear anyone, I swing it open all the way and make a run for it.

I force air in and out of my lungs as my pulse pounds in my ears, and I don't even consider what may happen to me if I get caught.

I speed walk down the hall and around the corner. I'm so close...so close...and that's exactly how far I get before running into a hard wall of muscle.

My hands fly up upon instinct, my palms landing against his chest. I jump back and retract my hands, as if touching Damon burns my skin.

"Didn't I fucking tell you to stay in my office?" He is furious. The look in his eyes is deadly, and I'm so scared, I think I might throw up. Everything about Damon sets off my fight or flight instincts.

"If you don't start listening to what I say, you're going to end up like your stupid brother."

All my fear transforms into fury, and in that moment of insanity, I slap Damon right across the face.

Pain sears through my hand, burning deep into my skin.

People down the hall stop their conversation and gawk, their eyes moving to where we stand. I take a chance and look up into Damon's dark gaze. Surprise flickers in his stare, but it quickly evaporates, leaving nothing but fury.

His hand comes up as if he's going to hit me, and I instantly try to get away. My legs stumble backward, and like the klutz I am, I manage to trip over my own two feet, landing on the unforgiving ground. Pain radiates up my spine as soon as my ass hits the floor. I groan, and just when I think the worst of my fall is over, an ache develops at the back of my head.

Pain lances through my body. I knew coming here was a bad idea.

"You're a pain in the fucking ass. A pain in the ass I have zero time or patience for. And now you've made a mockery out of me in front of my own people. You slapped me. You actually fucking slapped me." Damon's eyes are wild, and my vision blurs as I try to backpedal, but there's nowhere to go.

With the wall directly behind me, I'm at his mercy.

Without another word, he grabs me by the upper arm. His grip is harsh, and I know there will be bruises, but he doesn't seem to care. He doesn't give me a chance to get to my feet either. He starts walking, dragging me back toward his office. My head throbs, and a pounding begins behind my eyes.

"Apparently, you have a hard time following directions. I suppose I'll have to show you exactly what happens to those who don't follow my orders."

His tone is clipped, and when we enter the office again, he releases me, and my body sags against the floor. I try to stand back up, but I'm too dizzy and weak in the knees. I look up at him as he towers over me like an overlord.

"Don't fucking look at me like that," he snarls. His eyes are as dark as the midnight sky, and I'm frozen into place with fear. "When I tell you to do something, you do it."

I slither back across the floor, trying to put some distance between us, but he doesn't want distance—no, he wants to prove he's in control.

He reaches for his belt, and my insides twist.

"I own you now, and you'll do whatever I say when I say it. You'll do whatever the fuck I tell you simply because I fucking told you to do it. Your protection is not guaranteed, and right now, I'm considering killing you myself."

What the hell is he talking about? He owns me now? I'm too scared to ask...hell, I'm too scared to do anything right now. Just when I think this situation can't get any worse, he slides his belt from its loops, sending me into a full-blown panic attack.

I close my eyes, trying my very best to get my breathing under control, but the air won't enter my lungs. Fear is paralyzing me. I don't know why I'm so scared.

Actually...I do.

Damon.

My head is already spinning from the fall, and before I know it, I've been holding my breath too long. My lungs burn, and darkness closes in around me, dragging me deeper and deeper into an abyss.

amon

WHAT THE FUCK is wrong with this chick? I kneel in front of her crumbled body and examine her. Using my hands, I lift her head and feel for a wound. My fingers comb through her hair. The locks are smooth—so smooth, I envision tugging on them as I fuck her from behind. I blink, shaking the thought away.

No, you do not want to fuck her. You. Do. Not.

I make note of the large knot on the back of her head, then I inspect her face. Now I can see how pretty she is without the fearful expression on her face. Why the hell is she so scared of me?

I can't leave her on the floor. I slide one arm underneath her shoulders, and the other beneath her knees, then I pull her into my body, tucking her into my chest.

She feels perfect in my arms, her weight resting against me. Her head rolls toward me, and her face presses against my shoulder. Through the fabric of my shirt, I can feel her breath on my skin. It sends a shudder down my spine.

I'm about to lay her on the couch, but then stop. I enjoy holding her in my arms, and I decide to do so for a few more minutes.

Why? I don't fucking know.

She looks so peaceful. No scowl, no fear, no terror. Women look a lot of different ways when I have my hands on them, but peaceful has never been on that list.

My chest tightens and part of me, deep down, likes this—it likes it a lot.

Her eyelids flutter open, and two big brown orbs stare up at me. There is a split second before she recognizes who's holding her. A moment where that peacefulness and trust she had for me in her sleep is still apparent.

It passes, though, and fear returns to her beautiful chocolate-colored eyes. I wish the time between us wouldn't end, but when her body instinctively pulls away from mine instead of leaning into me for comfort, I place her ass back down on the couch beside me, noticing the slight tremble of her body.

"Are you going to fucking live or do I need to tell my guys to dig a grave outback?" I consider the fact that maybe scaring her more is not such a good idea...but hell, that's what I do best. Scare people...and kill them. You get one or the other.

"I want to go home, but most of all, I want to know what happened to my brother."

I think those are the most words she's said to me all day. Maybe that fall rattled some courage loose inside her head, but I can't have her going around asking questions.

"You will listen to me, Kiera, or you will die. This world isn't the same as yours. You're walking into a fucking nightmare. One wrong move will get you killed. Do you understand me?"

Tears roll down her creamy white cheeks. First one...then two... and for some reason, they gut me.

They rip me apart from the inside out.

"Tell me what happened to him?"

"First rule, don't ask questions. That's exactly the kind of thing I'm talking about. Questions like that will get you killed. Keep your mouth shut and do what I say, otherwise I'll find another job for your lips, and you don't really look like the sucking cock type."

Three knocks sound against the door, and I know who it is. When I see Hero enter the room, I sigh.

"Change your mind about the girl I offered?"

"No, I came to ask you for a ride home," he announces, clearly drunk off his ass from the way he falls into the chair at the front of my desk. I consider what he told me earlier, about Elyse, and how he loved her. The thought seems foreign to me.

Love doesn't exist in my world. It can't. It's a weakness that cannot be afforded. Because when you love someone, they become your Achillies heal. And your enemies...they'll use them against you any day.

"You think going home to your girl like this is a good idea?"

"No, but any other idea is shit too. Doesn't matter when I go home, my ass is still going to be chewed." I almost laugh. Trouble in paradise already.

"How about you crash at my place tonight? I've got something at home that will calm you down a bit without making you puke your guts out in the morning." I've been looking forward to smoking some weed all day, and Hero looks like he might need some as bad as I do.

"Sure, let's go then. I don't know how much longer my legs will work." They better work until he makes it to my couch 'cause I'm not going to carry his ass.

"Let's go, Kiera. Grab your shit, you're coming with me."

She hesitates for a moment, weighing her options. Her eyes flicker to the door like she's going to make another run for it. Instead, she grabs her backpack and gets up, her legs still unsteady. She better not faint again. Although, if she did, I would carry her.

I walk out the door ahead, both of them following me like lost sheep.

"How drunk am I?" Hero asks as we get in my car.

I wish he would shut up enjoy the damn ride.

"Pretty fucking drunk," I grit through my teeth. Looking into the rearview mirror, I see Kiera sitting in the back. She looks as if I'm driving her to her execution. What the fuck am I going to do with this girl at my house?

"Okay, good. Because I could've sworn there was a chick in the backseat of your car."

I almost smile at Hero's comment. Almost.

"Go to the guest room and lock the door behind you," I order Kiera, pointing her in the right direction. She scurries away, disappearing into the hallway like she can't get away fast enough.

Hero follows me into the living room and throws himself down onto the leather couch. I reach into a secret compartment in the end table and pull out a small metal case. Flipping it open, I take out one of the pre-rolled joints and put it between my lips.

Sitting next to Hero, I pull out a lighter from my other pocket and light the end of the joint. I suck in the sweet, calming smoke, filling my lungs as full as I can, just to puff it right back out. It takes about three drags before my body and mind relax, and I hand the joint over to Hero.

"So, you really are in love with that girl." I can't believe I'm even asking this question. Must be the weed. I hope Hero is fucked up enough to forget we ever had this touchy-feely conversation.

"So fucking much it hurts. I keep fucking up, but I can't help it. She pushes all my buttons, good and bad. It's driving me insane."

I nod at his explanation. I know all about someone pushing my buttons. She's sitting in the bedroom down the hall.

Halfway through the joint, Hero passes out, and I have to finish this bad boy myself. Oh well...

As soon as I reach a nice buzz and stop thinking about everything that annoyed me today, my phone vibrates in my pocket.

Of course, I start to chill out and everything goes to shit.

"What?" I answer without checking the screen.

Toni's voice comes through the line. "Hey, boss, sorry for calling so late, but I figured you might want to know about this right away." I have a feeling I most definitely do not want to hear anything he is about to tell me.

When I don't say anything, he continues. "The cleanup crew got back to me. They found some stuff on scene. It looks like Leo was working for Xander before they offed him. The way they killed him definitely proves it was his crew."

Fuck my life.

"Also, there was a note on the fridge. I'm sending you a picture of it now."

"Okay. I'll deal with this in the morning." I hang up the phone and look at the screen, waiting for the picture to come through. A few seconds later, it does. The words *We'll be back for you* are written in familiar handwriting on a sticky note. Suddenly, everything has taken a horrible turn.

Out of all the people in the world, did it have to be my stupid ass brother who was after Keira? Now, I do feel bad for her.

I lean forward and hold my head in my hands. Hero's soft snores fill my ears. If my brother gets his hands on her...I don't even want to think about it.

He'd break her. Destroy her. She might be scared of me, but she's never met Xander, and he's way fucking worse.

I've always hated Xander, even when we were kids. Probably because our father made us hate each other. I might be a dick, but Xander puts me to shame one-hundred percent. He's a psychopath without a caring bone in his body. Remembering my childhood and my crazy ass brother is not what I need to be doing right now. I can deal with all this shit tomorrow.

Pushing up from the couch, I walk over to the liquor cabinet and rummage through it. Vodka or Whiskey? I contemplate the choice like it's the only thing I should be concerned with right now.

My fingers wrap around the neck of the whiskey bottle, then I twist the cap off and pour myself a full glass. I can't even swirl the amber liquid around like I usually do because I've filled the fucking thing right to the rim.

Bringing the glass to my nose, I inhale. Smoke and wood fill my nostrils, along with an undertone of vanilla. I bring the glass to my lips and down half of it in one swallow, enjoying how it coats my throat with flames of fire, then settles deep into my stomach, warming my body all over.

I top off the crystal cup and take another large gulp, then another. Wiping at my mouth with the back of my hand, I wonder what kind of shit Leo was doing for my brother. My thoughts once again turn to Keira.

She is probably wondering why her brother would send her to an asshole like me. What she doesn't know is I'm way less of an asshole than the fucker who's after her. And her brother—well, he was right to send her my way simply because I'm the only one who can protect her from my brother.

I down the rest of the alcohol and make my way to my bedroom. The hallway is completely dark except a faint light escaping from beneath the guest bedroom door. I almost walk past it, but some invisible force makes me stop.

My mind starts to wander...

What's she doing right now? Is she sleeping? Is she naked? My cock hardens inside my pants. I lick my lips, thinking of all the different things I want to do to her.

Uh...fuck yes. She is probably naked in the bed.

Maybe I can sneak in and take a peek.

I know what I'm doing is wrong. I know it, but I don't give a fuck. I never said I was a gentleman...or a good man, for that matter.

It isn't until the doorknob turns in my hand and the door opens that I remember I told her to lock it.

I clench my jaw in anger.

Does this girl listen to a word I say?

I push the door open all the way and find her sitting on the bed, fully dressed.

Bummer.

I avert my eyes, refusing to look at her. She's beautiful, too beautiful, and I don't want to see her terrified gaze.

"You know, for someone who acts so fucking scared all the time, you really should improve your listening skills. You might make it out of this situation alive if you listen to me."

I walk up to the bed, and she scoots back to sit at the headboard, her legs drawn up to her chest making her appear even smaller than she is. The only thing she's taken off so far are her shoes. And like the sick bastard I am, I wonder what I'd have to do to make her lose some of her clothes. My dick grows harder thinking about the creamy bare skin hiding under all that fabric. I'd bet money she is soft all over...really fucking soft.

"You're going to do something for me, and you're going to do it because I told you."

Her eyes flash with fear. "And what is that?"

"Suck my cock."

Hugging her legs tighter, she whispers, "No."

I take a surprised step back. "No? You think I'm going to let you stay here...at my house...keep you protected...for free? It don't work that way, baby."

"I-I can leave." Her voice is soft and fragile—like everything else about her. I want to grab her by the shoulders, shake her, and yell. I want to tell her to swallow her fears and stop being so fucking weak.

"No, you can't, and you won't. The person who is after you, he's a real fucking prick. If he gets his hands on you, he is not going to be as nice as I have been." I keep my voice even and continue. "He is going to shove his dick down your throat and choke you with it before he beats the ever-loving fuck out of you. He won't offer you a place to live, or protection, and he definitely won't let you say no to him—not that it would matter if you said no. A hole is a hole."

I pause briefly, gauging Kiera's heart-shaped face. She looks worried, her tiny little body trembling against the headboard, leaving me with the visual of a million and one other ways I could make her tremble.

"So, if you want my protection, if you want me to shield you from him, you're going to get your sweet little ass over here and suck me off. After that, you're going to be a good little girl and listen to me, because I am so very fucking close to losing my patience with you."

I say the words, but I'm not sure I mean them. I can't force her to do anything she doesn't want to do. I can scare her. I can trick her, but there is no way in hell I'm taking something from Keira she doesn't want to offer.

eira

DAMON IS stands in front of the bed, swaying on his feet. He unbuckles his pants, and all I can think of is the woman's words from earlier today. *"Damon won't force you into something you don't want."*

Either she has no idea who she is working for, or I haven't made myself clear. Gathering up every ounce of courage I can, I lift my chin and repeat the word a little firmer this time. "No."

Damon's eyes darken, going real wide, and from the way he is looking at me, I know he wants to say something. There's a response on the tip of his tongue, and I'm not sure I want to know what it is. Thankfully, he doesn't say anything, and lets his hands fall to his sides.

"Suit yourself," he slurs before turning on his heels, storming out the room full of fury. He slams the door shut so hard, the lampshade on the bedside table shakes.

I listen to his footsteps as they disappear down the hall, then the sound of yet another door slamming somewhere off in the distance vibrates through me.

When he's completely out of ear shot, I let go of the pain and sadness. Every tear I held back today comes out all at once. Crying my eyes out, I curl up into the fetal position on the bed.

Sob after sob rattles my body, my chest heaving with unsteady breaths. My head starts to throb. It hurts so much, I feel as if I might puke. I remain this way for a long time, my heart shattering over and over again. I cry for the loss of my brother and the life I'll never have.

After what seems like forever, I finally cry myself into a restless sleep, hoping to escape this day, and that maybe when I wake up, this will all have been nothing more than a nightmare.

MY EYES FLY OPEN, and I gasp for air, desperately trying to fill my lungs. My heart beats so fast, it's about to come out of my chest. I wipe the sweat off my forehead, trying to calm myself, forcing the images of masked men killing my brother *and me* out of my head. I scurry across the unfamiliar mattress. It takes me a minute to get my bearings, but eventually, I rest at the edge, my head in my hands.

I am no stranger to night terrors, but this was so real, so intense. I can't go on much longer like this. This can't become my life.

Being scared every second of the day, only to close my eyes at night and deal with my nightmares when I should be able to escape this world at least for a short time. I can't live like this.

Damon might not force himself on me, but he also won't protect me unless I give him what he wants.

I swing my legs off the bed and creep out into the hallway. It's dark, dark as midnight. My hands feel along the wall until I find a light switch. My eyes squeeze shut from the brightness that fills the space. My gaze swings up and down the hall. There are four doors, two to the right and two to the left, and out of all of them, there's only one that's closed.

I feel anxious even walking across the hall toward it. It must be Damon's, though I suppose it could be that other man's?

Holding my breath, I twist the knob, opening the door as quietly as I can. I sneak into the room with treacherous tears upon my cheeks. Crying is a weakness to Damon, I know this, but I can't stop the emotional roller coaster I'm on. I sniffle into my arm and wipe away the tears. Then I glance up and take in every single inch of Damon Rossi.

He's breathtakingly beautiful—in a dark and tormented way. His nearly black hair is disheveled. His body is relaxed—and damn does he have a body. It looks like it's been chiseled from stone— each muscle and crevice drawing me in. His eyes are closed, his chest rising and falling in an even rhythm.

As I tiptoe toward his bed, I consider turning around and running back the way I came. The fear of what may happen to me without his protection keeps me rooted. I have to talk to him...and try to reason with him. It's the only way I'm going to make it out of this alive. I exhale, letting all the anxiousness out.

My eyes drift over Damon's sleeping body one last time, but once I reach his face, I realize he isn't sleeping anymore.

"What the fuck are you doing?" His voice is gruff, and full of sleep.

"I'll do whatever you want." My voice comes out cracked and raw sounding. "I'll give you a blowjob or whatever you want, but I want something in return. I want you to promise you'll protect me."

Damon's eyes bore into mine. They're darker than normal in the dim lighting. I shiver—out of fear or cold, I don't know.

Time stands still between us. Damon doesn't say anything right away. He only looks at me like he's trying to figure out if I'm really standing at his bedside or not.

I chew on my bottom lip. I'm not really sure what to do now. Is he waiting for me to make the first move?

My nerves are on edge. I've never done anything like this before. I'm just over eighteen, and my brother made sure no one ever had a chance to date or kiss me. I'm trying to recall images from a porn I once watched out of curiosity.

I climb onto the bed, grabbing the top of the black comforter. I start pulling the heavy blanket off him, but he snatches my wrist.

"No...no blowjob. I don't want to force you to do something."

For a moment, I panic. *No?* Does that mean he's retracted his offer? Is he not going to protect me anymore? If he doesn't want this, then what does he want? I'm seconds away from begging him for his help, from offering him anything I can think of.

Even my virginity... The very last thing I own.

He doesn't give me a chance to plead or beg for his protection. Instead, he does something that seems very unlike the Damon I've come to know. Releasing my wrists from his steel-grip, he pulls me on top of him. I can feel his hot breath against my lips, and I wonder if he's going to kiss me.

And then he does.

His full lips sear mine.

I can't think. I can't breathe. Fear trickles up my spine.

I'm kissing Damon. I'm kissing him. Or maybe he's kissing me.

I go stiff against him. My first thought is to push him away, but then I feel his soft, warm lips deepen against mine. He's a kisser..and my body starts to become affected by those real kisses, burning me up from the inside out.

An emotion so deep, something I've never experienced before, throbs to the surface, spiraling out of control inside me. My body softens into his hold while my lips mold to his. My lips were made to kiss his. He tastes like bourbon, and there's a faint smokiness clinging to his skin. It's an exotic combination, but I don't mind. All those things heighten our kiss. My fingers splay across his bare, chiseled chest, as if holding onto him could stop my body from melting into a pile of mush.

I feel him pull away slowly, his lips feather light against mine until he's completely gone. And like a flower misses the sun's warmth at night, I miss Damon's lips against mine. His warmth seeps into me, showing me a side of him I'd been certain didn't exist. My brown eyes bleed into his sleepy, coffee-colored ones. His gaze never wavers from mine, and I watch as something swims in his eyes—an unreadable emotion. Deep down, I know I'll be okay. I don't know how I know this or why, but I can feel it in Damon's gaze—like a protective blanket coating my body.

The moment ends, and with little effort, Damon pulls me to his chest. I rest my head against his warm skin. The sound of his heart beating fills my ears, its steady rhythm calming me. As his hands glide down my arms, goosebumps cover my skin.

After today, I was certain I'd never let him touch me again, but now I'm not so sure.

His hold on me tightens, instinctually, as if he wants to make sure I don't go anywhere. Shock twists deep inside me as he brings his other hand to my head, burying his thick fingers into my brown mane. When he starts playing with the natural curls at the ends of each strand, I nearly moan.

His touch relaxes me, soothes me. I don't want this moment between us to end.

"Don't be scared. You have no reason to be scared of me." He licks his lips before smiling at me. "I'm a bastard, a killer, and the worst man to be in your presence, but I'll do whatever I can to protect you," he whispers before his hand stills in my hair, cradling my head against his body.

His touch is gentle; his eyes are kind. This is the man I wish I'd met earlier today. Not the devil in disguise.

"Do you mean that?"

"Yes, I mean it."

He sounds like he is about to go back to sleep. Afraid to move, to wake him, I cuddle up to his warm chest, letting him comfort me, partially because it feels good, and partially because I know he's the only one who can now.

My eyes grow heavy, and I doze in and out of consciousness, though I never go fully back to sleep.

When I notice the sun rising, the first morning rays shining in through the window, I decide to get a shower. The only reason I didn't shower last night is because I was scared to take my clothes off even for a second with a guy like Damon under the same roof as me. Now that I feel a little better, and after the kiss that took place between us, I'm confident no one is going to jump me in the bathroom.

Least of all Damon.

I slowly peel myself off him. My cheek is hot where his chest touched my skin, and I run my fingers against it to draw some of the warmth out. As soon as I'm up and out of the bed, I immediately miss it. I miss him, the warmth, and the sound of his heartbeat beneath my cheek. It's a strange emotion to be feeling toward a man who had threatened to kill me not even twenty-four hours ago.

But after all I've endured, nothing can truly shock me. Not now. With one last fleeting gaze, I sneak back into the guest room, grab my backpack, and go into the attached bathroom.

After showering and dressing, I hear a loud commotion outside my door. The guy from yesterday—Hero, I think—runs out of Damon's room like a madman. His shoulder bumps into mine. Luckily, I'm close to the wall, otherwise I'd be sprawled out on the floor from the force.

Damon appears from his room a moment later, fully dressed, a look of annoyance on his face.

Where the hell are they going?

"Stay here, don't touch anything, and don't try to leave. If you do, I'll find you, and if you thought I was bad yesterday, you haven't seen a damn thing, sweetheart."

I gulp down my fear, attempting to hide the feelings he draws out of me. This is the guy I met at the club, not the one I saw last night in his room. Why is he acting this way? Why is he pretending to be someone he clearly isn't?

With his mask fully in place, he walks away, leaving me a mess of misunderstanding and confusion. I decide then that Damon might have everyone else fooled, but after getting a glimpse of him—the real him—I'm not sure I'll ever be able to see him the same again.

amon

WHEN I WENT to bed last night, I thought I'd had the equivalent of a shitty day. But fuck me sideways, today has been far fucking worse. In all the years I've been selling drugs, running Night Shift, and pimping girls out, I've never seen as much pain as I have today.

Hero is a friend, a damn good one, but seeing him find Elyse the way he did, the anguish in his eyes, the despair...it stabbed me in my nonexistent heart. I've seen my fair share of violence...hell, I've done most of the killing, but what I experienced today...I don't think there will be any topping that for a while.

Pulling into the driveway of my house, I realize Keira is still here, and that she's been here all fucking morning and afternoon alone.

Fuck! She may have ran. Fear swims through her veins all the time. It wouldn't surprise me if I found her gone.

My thoughts shift, remembering the look in her eyes last night as she let me pull her into my arms. She was scared, terrified, afraid of something. I don't know, I didn't bother asking, but I could see it in her eyes.

She wanted my protection, practically came begging me for it, and I promised her I'd give it to her without hurting her or demanding a damn blowjob.

Why did I turn her down? I grind my teeth together, as if doing so will draw an answer out of me. I don't fucking know why. Maybe it was the weed or the booze or the combination of the two that got the thing in my chest to work like I told it not to—or maybe I didn't want to see her beautiful face full of fear and stained with tears anymore.

I roll my eyes.

Stupid me. Stupid heart.

Sometimes, I wish the fucker would stop beating altogether. When your heart gets involved, it leads you down roads you normally don't go down. I could easily see Keira and her tiny, hot as fuck body guiding me down a road I don't need to go down.

I kill the engine on my Cadillac and get out, slamming the door. I still have to go back to the club, which means I have to go inside, corral Keira, then drive all the way across town with her in tow. And after last night, I know I'm going to get an earful. I need to make sure shit like last night never happens again.

I can't be seen as weak, especially not by her.

Walking up the front steps, I unlock the door and push it open.

My gaze swings around the open entryway. A part of me hopes she left—less work I have to do—while the other part is scared shitless at the thought. If my brother gets his grubby paws on her, she's as good as dead. Still, knowing I want her to be here more than I want her gone irritates the shit out of me.

She irritates the shit out me.

Her presence, and the fact that she makes me feel more emotions in one day then I've felt in my entire life.

As I move deeper into the house, I look around for her. Complete silence settles over each and every room. No TV or radio on. No running water, foot steps, or any other sounds that would give her being here away.

I clench my fists at my side. I hate how disappointed I am that she's gone, and I hate even more that I'm already making plans to find her.

I walk back into the living room and realize I've left the joint from last night on the coffee table. I lean over to grab it, and that's when I see her—her small body lying in the recliner. She's curled up in a blanket, her eyes closed and face relaxed, making her features even more beautiful. Her lips are slightly parted, and I'm reminded of the kiss we shared. I still don't know what came over me when I kissed her. All I know is I wanted to do it then, and I want to do it again right now.

Like the creep I am, I stand there, feet away, and watch her sleep. She's so at peace, so fucking perfect, it's insane. I wonder for a half-second what it would be like to have her as mine. As soon as the thought enters my mind, I shut it down.

I'm Damon Rossi. I don't do love. I don't do *mine*. Nothing lasts forever in the world I live in, and Keira is too weak to survive it.

But she's damn nice to look at. I don't know how long I stand there, staring, watching every breath that fills her lungs. The sudden ringing of my phone pulls my attention away from Keira, and I swear the damn ringtone has never been so fucking loud. Kiera practically jumps from the recliner, the blanket covering her moments ago hitting the floor. Her movements make me jump a little too.

I don't even check the caller ID. I hit ignore and stuff the phone back in my pocket. Whoever it is can wait. I have more important things to assess to right now.

"I have business to attend to at the club. Let's go."

Keira eyes me cautiously, as if I'm a rabid animal that could attack at any given second.

"Why do I have to go? I don't like it there." She frowns, still breathing heavy from being scared by my ringtone.

"This shit again?" I roll my eyes. "How many times do I have to tell you how this works? I order you to do something, and you fucking do it! No questions asked, no comments, no whining—a whole lot of actually fucking doing what I tell you." Fire burns through my veins. I'm not used to this shit, to people not doing as they're told, when they're fucking told.

I take a step toward her. This time, she doesn't scurry away from me. "I don't give a fuck what you like or don't like, Keira. If you want me to protect you even a little, you will start to listen to me. Now, put your fucking shoes on before I drag you out of here barefoot." She visibly gulps, but doesn't say anything. In fact, for fucking once, she listens.

We drive back to the club in silence. I watch her out the corner of my eye and can tell she's nervous by the way she fidgets with her hands in her lap.

A tiny smirk pulls at my lips. At least she's not as terrified as yesterday. I ponder if that's a good or bad thing. Part of me knows she would be better off being scared of me—like the rest of the people in my life.

The neon lettering of the Night Shift sign comes into view, and I tell myself I need to leave all my personal shit at the door. This is my place of business, and that's all it can be. People need to view me as the boss and nothing else. Weakness is not an emotion I can afford to show—not for anyone.

"Why a strip club?" she asks, breaking the silence as I pull into my parking spot. What a dumb question. Why not a strip club? What else would I open up? A fucking bakery? I ignore her question and cut the engine.

"Listen up, doll. We're going to go in there, and you're to follow behind me like I have a fucking leash around your neck. If you don't, I might actually put one on you. You are not to talk to anyone. Don't even make eye contact with anyone too long. Then you're going to sit on the couch in my office and look pretty. Don't fucking talk to me, and don't fucking talk to anyone who comes in to do business with me. You got all that?"

Her brown orbs blaze with fire.

Her anger makes my cock hard. I want to see her angry more.

She opens her perfect mouth to say something, but stops when I hold my finger to her plump lips. "I give an order...you do it! Nod if you got it."

She nods slightly, her lips trembling. There's still heat simmering in her eyes, but it's significantly diminished.

I turn, dismissing her, and get out of the car, waiting for her to climb out so I can lock it. Without looking back, I march through the back door and walk my usual round through the club. I know Keira is directly behind me, following like a lost puppy. I can feel people staring at us. They're probably wondering who she is and why the fuck she's following me around.

When they figure it out, maybe they can let me know. I don't even know why I still have her here with me.

When we finally get to my office, she sags down onto the couch and looks up at me with her beautiful brown eyes.

She looks a little pale. Her eyes are tired, and the way she's laying against the leather couch, she appears worn out. Suddenly, I wonder if she's had anything to eat all day.

"Have you eaten?" I huff. I'm still not used to caring for anyone but myself, so it seems strange to ask such a question.

"You told me not to touch anything."

My face falls, and fills with shock. "You gotta be fucking kidding me."

I pick up the phone and call the bar. Candy answers on the second ring, her sultry voice filling the receiver. "Night Shift."

"Candy, bring us some food...whatever the fuck the special is, and a beer. I need a fucking beer." My eyes lift to Keira. "Maybe bring Kiera a drink too. Whatever fucking girls drink." I slam the phone down, ending the call before she can respond.

My eyes find Keira's. Seeing her pale skin angers me so much. Why the fuck wouldn't she eat? Why wait until she's sick?

I shove the thoughts away before I blow my top, and busy myself with looking at pictures of possible new girls, but my eyes keep wandering back to Keira sitting on the couch like she's at the dentist's office waiting to be seen. Wearing yoga pants, sneakers, and a baggy white shirt, she couldn't look any more out of place —yet she still looks hot as fuck.

I don't understand my infatuation with her. She makes my blood run hot. Her inability to listen turns me on more than I care to admit.

A knock sounds against the door, and a moment later, Candy walks in, bringing us our food. She sets a bottle of my favorite beer in front of me and hands Keira some light pink colored drink with a little umbrella on the rim.

"I'm not old enough to drink," Keira says after Candy leaves. It reminds me that I don't know anything about her—let alone her age.

"How old are you?"

"I just turned eighteen." Well, at least she's legal.

"How old are you?" Her question takes me by surprise. I can't remember the last time anybody asked me such a mundane question.

"Twenty-two." I know I shouldn't have answered. The twinkle appearing in her eyes tells me she's eager to learn more about me, and I don't want her to ask any more prying questions.

"How long have you owned this place?"

Exactly what I didn't want to happen. More questions. I don't want her knowing more about me than she needs to.

"Enough questions. Eat. In silence."

Candy comes back a few minutes later to take our plates, and replaces my empty beer bottle with another.

Keira hasn't touched her drink, but her hands are wrapped around the glass like she's considering it.

"Dave is at the bar waiting for you to call him in," Candy announces, an unsure look on her face.

"Send him in."

Candy nods and leaves the office.

My gaze swings to Keira. "Remember what I said. Keep your mouth shut," I warn and watch her take her first sip of the pink drink.

A knock sounds on the door, and I call for him to enter. Dave walks in, his eyes going straight to Keira.

"Oooh, who is this? New girl?" The grin on his face tells me he's more than interested, and I don't like it—not one fucking bit. His eyes roam up and down her body, and images of me bashing his head into the side of my desk immediately enter my mind.

"Don't mind her. She's my new secretary. Getting her a tiny little desk for the corner soon," I mutter through a clenched jaw.

When his eyes continue to linger on her petite frame and heart-shaped face, I almost lose it. "Sit your fucking ass down and quit staring at her. You came here for business, not to eye-fuck my secretary."

Dave pales at my sudden outburst and sits in the chair in front of my desk without another glance at her.

"Tell me about business." I place my feet on the edge of the desk and listen to him drone on about how much he's been selling, in what areas, the new guys he hired, and how the cops got one of our guys in custody but he isn't talking.

The entire time he's speaking, my eyes wander to Keira. She's been silently taking small sips of her girly drink, her plump lips puckered around her straw. My dick is harder than hell.

"All right, that will be all," I interrupt. I stopped listening minutes ago, too enamored with Keira's lips around that damn fucking straw. Does she even realize what she's doing? Probably not, but I don't care. She can play innocent all she wants. I'll be the judge of how truly innocent she is.

"Out!" I yell when Dave doesn't move fast enough. He scurries out of my office, and I watch Keira take the last sip of her drink. She puts the empty glass down on a little side table next to the couch and looks at me with glassy eyes. Is she tipsy from one drink?

"How long has Dave been working for you?" Her stupid question only adds fuel to my fire—the inferno already burning out of control inside me.

I get up and step around my desk. Keira's eyes go wide when I stop in front of her and she sees the bulge in my pants.

"Get up!" I order. I'm so fucking tired of her questions. They're intrusive and unnecessary. She doesn't need to get to know me. She needs to learn to listen, to bend to my will—or I may just fucking break her.

She hesitates again, and I grab her by her silky, brown hair, my fingers digging into her scalp as I pull her to her feet. Her eyes, her lips, her body—all of it draws me in, begging me for things I'm not even sure it knows it wants.

A shriek of pain rips from her throat, and I shut her up with a searing kiss. Her hands land on my chest. I loosen my hold on her hair and pull her against me. I'm sure she's going to push me away, but she shocks me and grips my shirt, holding me close while I devour those sweet lips.

Our lips still locked, I manage to pull her to the couch, settling her on my lap. My hand grips her head, tilting it back, giving me access to her neck. I see her pulse throb, and I press a kiss to it. My lips roam over the sensitive flesh, and I use my free hand to move her hips, grinding her into my cock.

"My offer still stands. Sex and I'll protect you." I murmur into her ear, releasing my hold on her hair so she can look at me. Her eyes fill with confusion.

"Last night...you said..."

She tries to stand, but I hold her down, pushing her ass onto my hard length, letting her feel how much I want her. Knowing I could have her if I really wanted to, but that I won't, is driving me insane.

"Last night, I was drunk and high. I say a lot of shit I don't mean when I'm high. Now, what's it going to be? You going to spread those sweet legs for me willingly, or do you want your legs spread by someone else?"

Panic fills her eyes, and she tries to get up again. This time, I let her. As soon as she's out of my lap, hate and disgust fill her eyes. The way she's looking at me right now knocks the wind from my lungs. I open my mouth to say something, anything, but she runs out of the office, slamming the door behind her before I can get to her. I push the tightening of an emotion I don't understand inside my chest away. I don't bother following her. What's the point? I told all my guys not to let her leave, and unlike her, they know better than to disobey me.

As I sit a moment longer, my cock throbbing with need, I realize Keira is an itch I can't fucking scratch. She'll never give herself up to me—never—and that bothers me a lot. But if I can't have her, I'll have someone else.

I need a blowjob right fucking now. That might fucking help me. Maybe it'll get Keira out of my head. I think about it a second longer. I actually need fucking more than a blowjob, but I'm a little unhinged at the moment and don't want to hurt anyone, so I suppose I'll just go for a blowjob.

I pick up the phone again and dial the bar. "Send Hayley to my office *now*," I growl into the line when Candy picks up, then I slam the phone back down and wait.

Two minutes later, I'm leaning back in my office chair while Hayley kneels in front of me, her pink painted lips wrapped around my dick, worshiping it like it's a fucking god. She sucks hard and fast, and I close my eyes, enjoying her skills, wondering how much sweeter Kiera's lips would feel wrapped around my cock instead.

7

eira

I'm angry. At myself. At the situation. I thought Damon was better than the man he just proved himself to be. How could I be so stupid? I knew he wouldn't force me. I knew it, but that didn't make his advances any less scary.

I wander aimlessly around the club trying every single exit Damon and I walked past earlier. Every single one has a bouncer standing in front.

Am I a prisoner now?

I notice people's stares, how their eyes linger on me just a little too long. It leaves an uneasy feeling in the pit of my stomach. I don't look like any of the other girls here. In fact, I stick out like a sore thumb. I tuck a couple strands of hair behind my ear as I continue to survey the club. The staff watches me curiously, as if they don't get Damon's obsession with me. I want to tell them I don't get it either, but I keep my mouth shut. I want to get out of here as soon as possible, and without making trouble for myself.

A couple strippers sneer at me as I walk past the dressing rooms, but they don't say anything—which I'm thankful for. The club is open now, and I notice some men sitting around the center stage.

I see one of the strippers working the pole. She's wearing nothing but a thong, her tits bouncing with every movement she makes. My cheeks heat at the image, and I avert my eyes. When one of the guys turns his attention to me, looking me up and down, I decide I've had enough searching for the day.

It's painfully obvious no one here is going to let me leave, and after the way that guy stared at me like he wanted to eat me alive, there is no way I'm staying in this room, so I leave my pride behind and make my way back to Damon's office.

He might be a monster, but I get the feeling there're darker bastards lurking in the shadows here.

I walk swiftly down the hall and stop directly in front of Damon's door. I twist the knob, opening it with ease, and instantly regret not knocking. Damon is behind his desk, leaning back in his chair, his eyes closed and arms behind his head. His features are full of pleasure. And as my gaze moves lower, I notice a head with long blonde hair bobbing up and down on his lap.

Oh my god, not on his lap...his cock.

She's giving him a blow job.

My eyes bulge, the air in my lungs stills, and I swear I can hear my own heartbeat in my ears.

I don't know who I hate more right now—him for being such an ass, or her for giving him a blowjob. Or maybe I should hate myself for feeling jealous.

Damon's eyes open a moment later and find mine like a magnet. "Ahhh, Kiera...want to join in the fun? I'm sure Hayley could give you a lesson or two, teach you the way around a dick." The smug look on his face makes the whole situation worse. He tips his head back in pleasure, a moan escaping his full lips—lips I kissed not long ago. My hands shake, and bile begins to rise in my throat.

I can't look at them another second.

I need to get out of here. I need to find some way to leave.

Slamming the office door for a second time tonight, I scurry back down the hall, tears threatening to escape. I try my best to blink them away, refusing to cry over Damon. He doesn't care about me or my safety. He just cares about making me *his*, controlling me. I hate this place, and maybe even Damon.

Everything about him reminds me of a prison, and I want to escape—need to escape. He doesn't intend on protecting me, so why am I still here?

You have nowhere else to go, idiot.

I huff out a breath and walk down the hall, unsure of what to do. I'll have to wait for the perfect moment to escape, for one of the bouncers to take a break or something—which basically means I'll have to watch as many of them as I can without drawing too much attention to myself. Until then, I'll just walk around the bar and try to blend in. I almost laugh. I'm not dressed in sexy clothes. I look like I belong in a nunnery. There is no way in hell people aren't going to notice me.

I move slowly out onto the floor while scanning the exit doors. Then I finally see it: my chance, my out. One of the guys at the side door leaves his post and walks up to the bar. He starts telling Candy something, and she laughs, but I don't wait around to see what he plans to do or say next. This might be my only chance.

Trying not to run or draw any attention to myself, I move toward the door. A nervous sheen of sweat coats my hands. Every step, I expect someone to grab me from behind and drag me back to Damon's office. My body trembles as I reach the door. My hands rest against the heavy metal, and as I push it open, I nearly pass out. When the outside air hits my lungs, I sigh in relief. I can't believe I actually made it outside.

I glance over my shoulder, assuming someone is surely going to come through that door at any second and run after me. After a few moments, I realize no one seems to have paid me any attention. I let the heavy, metal door shut behind me and make my way into the parking lot. Only then, with my newfound freedom surrounding me, does something occur to me: I have no phone, no money, and no place to go.

What the hell am I going to do?

"Keira?" I turn at the familiar voice, and blink, shocked to see the one person I never expected to see here. Lily Baker. My lab partner and close friend. She stands about five feet away staring at me, looking completely confused. Probably as confused as I am.

"Lily!" I look at her like she's an angel sent to me from God—and maybe she is. I close the distance between us and take her into a fierce hug. "Oh, Lily, you have no idea how good it is to see you right now." I wonder if she can tell how sad I am. How exhausted I am.

"Keira, what are you doing here?"

Oh god, what am I going to tell her? I could ask her the same thing, I suppose.

"I've had a rough couple days. I—I honestly don't want to talk about it right now. Anyway, what are you doing here?"

She doesn't bat an eye. "I'm here with Gunner." She points her thumb over her shoulder, and only then do I realize there's a guy standing a few feet behind her.

"Oh, hey." I give him a small wave, but can't even bring myself to force a friendly smile. All I want is to get out of here, away from here, as far away as I can get. I'm sure Damon will feel the same relief to be rid of me when he discovers I'm gone.

"Are you here with someone?" Lily asks softly, her eyes peering into mine.

"No, I'm alone." I almost break down and cry, realizing just how true that statement is. I am alone...so fucking alone.

"Do you need a ride somewhere? We were just about to leave."

Gunner grunts behind her, and I'm certain he doesn't want me to tag along with them. Then again, I don't understand why he's hanging out with Lily anyway. Last I knew, they hated each other.

"Sure, I...actually, I don't really have a place to go to right now." I pause. "I mean, my brother just passed away, and I don't really want to be alone right now." I'll take Lily's pity, so long as it gets me away from Damon.

"Oh, Keira...is that why...you're here?" Her gray eyes soften as she looks at me like she just put some puzzle pieces together. She couldn't be more wrong, but I figure this is easier than telling her what I'm actually doing here. So I let her believe I'm here to strip.

I nod my head, lowering my eyes to the ground in shame.

"Why don't you come with me tonight? You can crash at my place, and tomorrow, we can figure something out." Lily wraps an arm around me and pulls me into her side. Her touch is kind, calming. She's a good friend. I want to tell her there's no figuring out my problems, but the thought of getting away even for a night is too tempting.

If I have to lie, then I will. I've already partially lied, so what is the harm in another?

"Okay. That would be great." I force a smile. I feel eyes on me, and notice Gunner's dark gaze. He'll just have to deal with it. I'm not scared of him, not as much as I am of the man inside those walls behind me. There is no way in hell I'm passing up the chance to get out of here.

"All right. Let's go." Lily smiles, and for the first time in days, I feel like everything is going to be okay.

8

amon

As soon as I step outside my office, I know she's gone. I don't know how to fucking explain it, but this strange sensation overtakes me. I should've been more focused on her instead of getting my cock sucked. But it was either get my cock sucked, or have her do it, and something told me she wasn't going to do it.

Keira is like a kitten—if you hold her down, she will scratch and bite you until you release her, and I kind of like that about her. What I don't like is she can't follow the damn rules—even if they are to protect her.

I stomp down the hall, out to the packed bar and dance floor. Music blasts through the speakers as girls dance on stage. Money flies through the air, and men call out to the women, begging them to fuck them. All is running as it should...and I guess that's one less thing for me to worry about.

I spot Candy working the bar. I feel calm, relaxed even, as I make my way to her—until the realization hits me: little fucking Keira escaped again. I'm done with her not obeying my orders. I've let this slide too many times. This time, I will show her a lesson, one she will never forget. I will have to hurt her to prove my point.

Leaning over the bar top, I motion for Candy to come over. She eyes me cautiously, almost as if she's afraid, and she has reason to be. She's been working here long enough to know when I'm in an explosive mood.

"Have you seen Kiera?"

"She was walking around here a while ago just looking around, eyeing the back doors. I haven't seen her for a while. I thought she went back to your office."

Motherfucking fuck. Of course she slipped through the cracks. She might stick out like a sore thumb, but she could make herself invisible if need be.

"Did anybody leave their positions, even for a moment?" I crack my neck, ready to beat someone's ass.

Candy doesn't say anything, but I see her eyes flash to where Diego is standing. I turn around, heading straight for him. As soon as he sees me coming, his face goes pale. He is a big guy, but I'm bigger...not that it matters. He wouldn't dare retaliate, not if he values his life.

I don't even stop to ask questions. I swing and hit him square in the jaw. His head snaps back, but—props to him—he doesn't pass out. Which is good. I still need him to man the door.

"What the fuck is more important than doing your job?"

"Nothing, boss."

Clenching my fist, I pull it back before slamming it into his nose. He grunts, but remains standing. Blood trickles down his nose and over his lips, but he doesn't dare make a move to wipe it away.

I grip Diego by his shirt and lean into his face. "Lie to me again, and I'll cut out your fucking tongue. I trusted you to guard this door. You know the rules, and I expect better from you."

Diego swallows and nods his head as if he understands. Well, maybe if his head wasn't in the fucking clouds, I wouldn't have to go searching for Keira.

Without another word, I march back to my office, feeling eyes on me. Slamming the door shut behind me, I get out my laptop and pull the surveillance tapes up. As I comb through four different screens, I spot her. Her silky brown locks and perfect body. I watch as she walks around the floor, eyeing the doors for a weak spot. Diego leaves post, and the light bulb inside her head turns on. She slips out the door and appears on another screen, an outside camera.

As I stare at the screen, I realize she's not alone.

Who the fuck is the girl she's with?

They talk like they know each other, which makes me wonder if Keira called her. Then I realize who is standing behind them. Gunner.

He's one of my bookies for the college, and now he's got something in his possession that is fucking mine. Clenching my teeth, I watch them get into Gunner's car and drive off.

I take a calming breath, trying to get my temper under control. If I don't, I'll seriously hurt Keira when I get my hands on her, and that's the last thing I want to do. If anything, I just want her to listen to me. Her brother sent her to me for a reason. She doesn't have to like it, but she has to follow my rules—and if she doesn't want to, maybe I should just wrap her up in a tight little bow and send her off to my brother.

My stomach lurches at the thought. Yeah, that's not going to fucking happen.

While I'm already on my laptop, I pull up Gunner's address from my files and punch it into my phone. If Gunner knows she belongs to me and took her anyway, I'll have no choice but to put a bullet in his brain.

I slam my laptop shut, lock up my office, then head out back and get into my Cadillac. The faint smell of strawberries enters my nostrils. My car smells like her...my fucking car. Is there anything this girl isn't going to take over? It feels like she's under my skin, inside my head. I grip the steering wheel hard, turning the ignition on and throwing it into drive. As I follow the directions to Gunner's place, I'm already thinking of ways to make her pay for leaving again. I hate that she's pushing me like this, forcing my hand.

After tonight, she won't leave again. I'll make sure of it.

The punishment will fit the crime.

I pull up to the curb, parking directly in front of his place. I stare out the window at the house, wondering if I'm in the right place. There's a white picket fence and flowers out front. The lawn is well-manicured, and I'd bet anything there is a BMW and 2.5 kids inside.

This place looks more like a single-family home than a college student's.

I exit the car, my jaw clenched, anger burning through me. I walk up to the door, trying to rein in my anger, but I know I'm too far gone.

I feel this overpowering urge to punch something or someone. I clench and unclench my fists, attempting to overcome the urge to kick down the front door.

Ringing the doorbell, I wait patiently...well, as patiently as I can, my fingers gripping the doorjamb.

The door opens moments later, and Gunner's surprised face appears behind it. Before he can mutter a single syllable, I push the door open all the way and force entry into the house. I don't give a fuck who owns this place. I take a couple steps forward, and as soon as I come around the corner, I see her.

Sitting on the couch is the other girl from the video—the one I don't know. She and Kiera look to be deep in conversation.

That's going to fucking end—right now.

Keira's eyes go impossibly wide when she spots me.

She jumps up from the couch, and yells, "I was going to come back."

Ha, sure you were.

I smirk, shake my head, then pull my gun from the back of my pants and hold it to my side. I don't want to point it at her, but I need her and Gunner to know I mean fucking business.

Gunner moves past me and positions himself between me and the other girl.

Is he protecting this other girl?

I don't fucking know. My mind is whirling; my only thoughts are on getting Keira back.

"Damon, boss, we...I mean...I...I didn't know she was with you."

Looking into his eyes, I know he's telling the truth. He had no idea.

"And that's the only reason there isn't a bullet in your brain right now. But if I ever find out otherwise, if I find her again, with either of you, you and the girl hiding behind you—you are dead." I look into the girl's eyes, making sure she gets the message as well.

"On second thought, she looks innocent as fuck, so I might just kill you and auction your girl off to the highest bidder." Gunner's entire body tenses. He wants to say or do something, but he knows better. He knows to keep his mouth shut when his boss is fucking talking, unlike someone...

I'm about to order Keira to get out, but she is already moving toward me, looking like she is about to attack me. Then she does —and I almost laugh.

I mean, I guess if you can call hitting my chest with her palms attacking me. She's weak, and her slaps do nothing but feed the burning inferno inside me.

She's never seen me angry, not like I am tonight. Tonight, she'll be wishing she would've stayed at the fucking club. I tuck my gun back while Keira keeps hitting me.

"I fucking hate you!" Her voice cracks at the end.

"Good, because your hate for me is only going to grow as the night goes on." I bend down and grab her by the waist, tossing her over my shoulder like she weighs nothing, and she doesn't— not really.

Gunner's girlfriend looks like she is about to come for me too. At least she seems to be a loyal friend—I'll give her that. Gunner stops her in her tracks, making her visibly angry. He leans down and whispers something in her ear, and I'm sure he's warning her, telling her the consequences of fucking with me.

Of course, Keira makes a scene and continues yelling at me while hitting my back with her tiny-ass hands. Her attack is futile. I'm not letting her go, and I'm not putting her down until we get to the car. When we get to the house, I'll tie her to the bed, making certain she can never escape.

"Goodbye, Gunner," I holler, then walk right out the front door, bouncing Keira against my shoulder, listening as the air leaves her lungs every time she falls back down.

She can't talk if she can't breathe, right?

"Put me down. It's not like you care anyway. You were getting a blowjob. You wouldn't have even known if someone came and got me."

I can hear the anguish in her voice. Is she jealous because Hayley gave me a blowjob, or afraid I won't protect her?

It sounds like she's jealous, and that makes me smile. If she's jealous, that means she might take me up on my offer. Then again, she probably won't. She's a fighter. A kitten with claws.

"It sounds like someone's jealous, but you don't have to worry about that tonight. Tonight, I'm all yours, baby. And just to prove a point, so you don't run again, I'm going to take that pretty little thing between your legs—and I'm going to enjoy every single second of it."

Her body shakes in my hold and I open the back door, tossing her against the bench seat of my car. If she thought I was a vicious bastard before, she has no fucking clue what she is in for.

I'll show her what happens when Damon Rossi's mercy runs out.

I drive home, clutching my steering wheel so tightly, the thing is in danger of ripping off. It takes everything inside me not to turn around and scream at her. So fucking what I was getting a blowjob. I was getting one because she refused to give me one, because she is nothing but a cock tease.

I hear her quiet sobs from the backseat, but I don't give a fuck right now. This is her own fault. She should have listened to me.

Fuck...she should have listened. The idea of hurting her doesn't sit well with me, but I have to do this. I have to prove I mean business. I've killed men for less; she can't keep getting away with this behavior.

The drive home is short, and when I turn into the driveway, I park inside the garage. My mind is still running rampant with anger. I can't think of anything besides showing her the conse-quences of what happens when you disobey me. I get out of the car, but she makes no move to open the back door. I guess I'll be a gentleman and do it for her. Reaching in, I grab her arm and pull her from the back seat. She whimpers in my hold, but I ignore it. I slam the door shut, drag her into the house, her feet digging into the floor the entire way to her room, then throw her onto the bed.

When I pull the handcuffs from my back pocket, she scurries away from me, but she's not fast enough—not to get away from me. I snatch her ankle and pull her back to the center of the bed.

"Please, Damon..." she pleads, tears in her big brown eyes.

I swallow down any and all emotions I feel for this woman, letting the anger continue to flow through my veins. I grab one of her arms and secure the handcuffs to it, then I pull her whole body up to the headboard and attach the other cuff around one of the bars.

With one hand cuffed to the bed, she can kick and scream all she wants, but she isn't going anywhere. I stand up, looking down at her like she is some kind of offering.

Undoing my belt, I watch her whole body shake and her face contort in fear while I unzip myself pushing the dress slacks down until my rock-hard cock is free and my pants are on the floor, kicked away from my feet. "Give me one good reason why I shouldn't do this. Why I shouldn't fuck you right now."

She looks up at me a moment, and I don't think she is going to say anything at all, but then she does—and just like the rest of her body, her voice is shaking too.

"Because you don't really want to hurt me." The tears stain her cheeks.

Don't I? I consider her words. I've been so consumed by rage since I found out she left, this might be the first time I actually stop to think. I need her to listen to me. I need her to be scared of me, but do I want to make that happen by hurting her? It's the only way I know how.

Do I really want to break her like this? Because that's what I would do if I hurt her this way. I'd break her, and I can't picture myself doing that to her.

Watching tear after tear roll down her face and onto the pillow is starting to bother me more than I care to admit. I can feel the anger starting to leave my body, leaving me with feelings I don't want or need. I can't look at her face anymore—I just fucking can't.

Grabbing her ankles, I flip her over onto her belly and pull her pants and underwear down in one go. Her cries are muffled by the pillow, but I can still tell her crying is getting worse. She starts to sob, her body shaking violently.

I squeeze my lids shut. I can't take it any longer. Her pain is starting to become my own, and I can't take it. I just fucking can't.

I lean over, tilting her head a little so I can see part of her face again. Brushing some tear-soaked hair from her cheek, I lean closer and whisper right into her ear.

"If you listen to me and be very still, I won't hurt you...and I won't take your virginity."

Her sobs almost stop immediately. Only small tremors she can't control remain. I stand up and look at her perfect body. Her skin is just as delicate and beautiful as I imagined it would be.

Creamy, white, unmarred. She's a specimen I want to explore over and over again. Her ass is plump, and each cheek jiggles as her body continues to shake.

"I'm going to touch you, but I won't hurt you." Starting at her ankle, I trail my fingers up her legs—all the way to the two perfect globes of her ass. The feeling of her warm skin on mine...there is no way to fucking describe it. God, she is beautiful, and pure, and fuck...I don't deserve her—not at all.

"I want to taste you, Keira. Can I taste you?" I wait patiently—as fucking patiently as I can for her to answer. Time seems to stand still, and when a breathless, "Yes," escapes her lips, I nearly come undone. Every muscle in my body, inside and out, tightens.

If I'm going to make her come, then it's going to be when I can see her fucking face. I want to see the pleasure in her eyes, the way she reacts to my touch. I retrieve a key for the handcuffs and undo them with ease, then I flip her over onto her back. When I see her face, I almost punch myself.

She looks sad, angry, and tired...and I never want to see her look like this again. I need to take care of her. I don't know why or how I'm going to do it, but I have to.

I crawl onto the bed slowly, all the anger seeping out of me, leaving me with nothing but the need to pleasure her—to make her feel the same insane need she makes me feel every single hour. Her eyes never leave mine, not even as I pull her to the edge of the bed. With my knee, I open her legs, and the sight of her pink pussy makes my mouth fill with saliva.

My eyes dart back up to hers, and I catch her watching me curiously, gazing at me, inspecting my every move.

I dip down between her legs and press a kiss to the top of her mound. Her legs widen, and a shiver rolls through her, and I love it. I fucking love that this is how she reacts to my touch.

Most of the time, I'm not the giving type, but with Keira, I want to be all that and more...so much more.

With two fingers, I spread her silky, smooth folds, revealing her tight little nub. My gaze trails down to her pussy, and I know I'll have to wait to claim that, but the need is definitely there, deep in my belly.

Exhaling, I lean forward and blow against the tender flesh. She shudders for the first time today with pleasure instead of fear, and I smile.

Without warning, I start licking her, flicking my tongue gently against her most sensitive part. A quiet moan rips from her throat, encouraging me to lick faster and harder. I look up at her, over her perfect pussy, to gage her facial features. Her eyes are closed now, but I want her to open them and look at me. I want to see the pleasure in her eyes.

I close my lips around her tight little bundle of nerves and start to suck lightly. Her body starts to respond to me. Her hips move probably without her even realizing it. Her body wants me, and just knowing that drives me insane.

Her lids finally flutter open, and I catch her looking down at me through hooded eyes. Her face is still red and puffy from crying, and she is the most beautiful woman I've ever seen. I suck on her clit a little harder this time and her eyes close again. Her head falls back onto the pillow, her moans growing louder and louder with every lick.

Her hands fist the sheets, and I know she's getting close. I keep working her clit with my tongue, watching her body move beneath me, begging for more without any words.

I lift one of her legs and rest it against my shoulder, opening her up wider—like she is a present I can't wait to unwrap. Her back arches off the bed.

"Damon..." she cries out, my name falling from her lips.

I need to hear her say it again. I might fucking die if I don't.

Her pussy quivers, and the taste of her sweet cream explodes against my tongue as she comes apart beneath me. I keep stroking her gently—up and down, up and down—tasting her over and over again, until I know every last tremor of her orgasm has moved through her body.

Gliding up her tiny form, I watch her eyes follow my every move. Indescribable desires pool deep inside me, and I have to see the rest of her naked. I grab the hem of her shirt and start to peel it off her body. She doesn't try to stop me, and instead, lifts her arms to help without me having to ask. Very slowly, I pull the shirt over her head, then unhook her bra and remove it, revealing two perfect tits with dusky pink nipples just begging to be sucked. Her tits are the perfect size, one handful each.

I lean down to take one of those perky tits into my mouth, but Keira stops me by tugging on my shirt, silently urging me to take it off. I sit up just long enough to pull it over my head, before tossing it to the ground behind me.

Then I'm back on top of her, taking that soft pink nipple into my mouth, making her moan again. I feel my cock growing harder and harder with each flick of my tongue against her pebbled nipple.

She's mine, all fucking mine. Her sweet strawberry scent urges me onward, and I want to take her—fuck do I want to take her—

but she's not ready for that yet. When I do get to feel her warmth wrapped around my dick, it's going to be because she wants it, because she begs for it.

Another soft moan escapes her mouth, and I want to bottle up those moans and keep them with me all the time. They are the sweetest fucking thing I've ever heard. She moves underneath me, rubbing her leg against my dick, and damn is he begging for attention.

"I want to feel you," I croak against her nipple, releasing it with a loud pop. I watch her chest rise and fall, her creamy white skin turning a soft pink right before my eyes.

"Okay." Keira nods, and I reach down, fisting my cock in my hand. It's heavy with need, and I wonder if she'll be able to take all of me when the time comes. She's so small, and I'm fucking huge—the two things just don't go together.

Her beautiful eyes go wide with fear for a moment, and I realize I need to clarify what I want and what I'm going to do.

"Don't be afraid. I'm going to bring my cock to your entrance, but I won't go in. I just want to feel you. Feel your slit, feel your pussy quiver against my cock."

"Okay," she repeats "But please don't go inside."

Her voice is so fucking soft, sweet and trusting, it hurts. I don't understand how she can still trust anything I say after what I've put her through the last two days.

I can't fuck this up. I can't lose control right now. Still fisting my dick, I bring myself right to her entrance. Her sweet pussy is still wet and so fucking soft, I want to plunge right inside her and never leave, claim her for myself—but I don't.

Instead, I let my cock move upward, sliding between her wet folds and over her clit. She exhales a ragged breath as I thrust forward between her folds, my cock maintaining friction against her clit.

Her still overly sensitive flesh glistens against the head of my cock. And its the most amazing feeling I have ever felt in my entire life, sliding through her silky wet folds. It's better than any sex I've ever had. Better than any killing I've ever done. I know I could come right now if I wanted to, but I need to savor this moment...draw it out as long as I can. Maybe even make her come again. I loosen the grip on my dick a little.

"You going to come again on my cock?"

"Yes...I think so..." Her breath hitches in her chest.

"Fuck yes you are..." I clench my jaw and move a little faster, feeling the tightening in my balls. Kiera's fingers splay against the sheets, as if she's reaching for something...needing something more.

I keep my rhythm the same and trail my fingers up her body, taking her puckered nipple between two fingers. I roll the nipple back and forth, watching as her eyes close, her hips lift, and her body shakes with an impending orgasm. There's nothing like the little gasps escaping her lips as she falls apart for me.

Goosebumps prickle across her skin, and I lean forward, my body looming above hers. My lips find hers, and I up my pace, my cock begging and pleading to be inside her.

Not yet, big boy.

I pull back and fist my cock in my hand, pumping the fuck out of him, feeling the burning pleasure rip through me. Seconds later,

I fall apart, my feet digging into the mattress and my heartbeat pulsing in my ears. I look down, watching as my release coats her virgin pussy, ropes of my sticky cum claiming her body as mine—only mine.

Another man will never have her, never touch her or taste her like I did tonight. If anybody tries, I'll slit their fucking throat.

My orgasm rocks me to the core. It's so fucking intense, it takes me a minute to gather my thoughts and get up.

"Don't move," I tell her softly, almost smiling. She doesn't look like she could move a fucking inch right now even if she tried. Moving away from the bed, even though I don't want to, I go into the bathroom and get a warm washcloth.

I reappear a few moments later and spread her legs, cleaning her perfect pussy that I made so fucking messy. Tossing the washcloth to the floor behind me, I crawl into the bed with her and pull her naked body into my chest, relishing in the way she shudders against me.

"You're mine, Keira. Mine. I don't care what you or anyone else thinks. After what happened between us tonight, I can't just let you go. I can't." My admission shocks the hell out of me as well as Keira, from the shocked expression she gives me.

She shifts slightly to look up at me. "Do you really mean that? Like...really mean it? Because seeing you with that stripper today...it hurt me."

Her creamy white cheeks heat. She seems embarrassed, and I don't understand why.

"I'm confused about how I feel. I don't want to like you, but I do. Or at least I like you when we're alone together...like this."

"I can't always be this person. People rely on me. I have to show a certain amount of hardness. I have to be a prick because I need people to be scared of me, and I have to do things you may not always like. At the end of the day, I'm still a criminal, baby."

And I don't know how to do this...any of it. Relationships are not for me, but I can't just have Keira as a fuck buddy.

"So, you're saying you are not really a prick? You just pretend to be one?" She gives me a smile, full of teeth and pure happiness.

"No, I'm definitely a prick, and I'll always be one." I pause for a moment, gathering my thoughts.

"What I'm saying is I don't have to be a prick with you...when we are alone. Other than that, I can't promise anything. I can work on my emotions, on how I treat you in the presence of others, but I can't promise you anything. I'm not a good man, Keira. I'm not, and I won't pretend to be, not even for you."

Keira doesn't say anything for a few minutes, and I wonder if she fell asleep. Then she sighs, and asks, "Will you see her again?"

I blink. "Will I see who again?" I whisper into her hair, inhaling her scent. Our scents have mixed together. I can't tell where she ends, and I start.

"Her. The stripper."

I contemplate my response. I'm a man, and I have needs, but Keira may be the one to curb those needs.

I imagine how she felt seeing me with Hayley. I really didn't think about it before. Putting myself in her shoes...I can't imagine how I would have felt if I would have caught Keira with another guy. The mere thought leaves me furious. I would have cut his heart out of his chest before he even had a chance to pull up his pants.

"Not if you don't want me to..." I tiptoe around my response. I don't want to hurt Keira—not anymore. "I want you, and I'd rather it be you, but..." I trail off, unsure of what to say. I can't image touching another woman now, not after touching her.

"I want to give myself to you. I'm just scared. Could we kind of work up to it? I told you I'd give you something in return for your promise to protect me."

I shake my head, holding her tightly against my chest. "No, Keira. I want you because you want me. Not because you want my protection. I'll protect you either way, because no one is touching you. No one. But if you want to give yourself to me, if you want me to fuck you because you want it, then I will—when you're ready."

The words don't even sound like something I would say, but then again, I'm not the same man I was an hour ago. Keira has cracked something inside me—she's opened up my heart. Now I understand what Hero was saying about Elyse. I can't imagine someone telling me I couldn't have Keira.

"So, we're okay?" Keira whispers, her voice sounding sleepy, and I realize how late it must be.

"More than okay, baby. More than okay." I kiss her softly, my lips melting against hers. I'm pretty sure I'll want her this way forever—which scares the hell out of me. In my world, love is a weakness—and weaknesses aren't something I can afford.

eira

FOR THE FIRST time in days, I wake refreshed. My body feels relaxed instead of tense. I sink into the soft mattress, my eyes opening lazily. Then I realize I'm not in *my* bed, but Damon's. His heavy arm is wrapped around my midsection, protecting me like a thick, steel band, holding me to him.

I'll never admit it aloud, at least not right now, but feeling this close to Damon, feeling his possessiveness, sparks something inside me. Something I don't really understand. It's a foreign emotion, but one I want to feel again and again. I let my mind wander to the things he said to me last night. Damon wants to be kind to me—and above all he can be—which tells me he's not really the twisted asshole he makes himself out to be.

I shift against the mattress, my eyes raking over his chiseled body. We're still naked. Our bodies molded together perfectly. I consider letting Damon be my first. He's never truly hurt me—not really—and he won't let anything happen to me.

His touch was exhilarating, powerful but gentle, and brought me immense pleasure. I nibble on my bottom lip, wondering what kind of pleasure his cock could bring me. He's been with plenty of women, and the thought disgusts me—but it is what it is. I can't expect him to have been chaste because I'm a virgin.

A shiver moves through my body as my eyes slide over his perfect V. It's well defined, and honestly, I'm not sure why Damon is so ripped. Maybe it's from all the torturing and body burying he does. Or maybe he secretly works out in his free time. Either way, I'm not complaining.

My mouth waters at the tent that starts to form beneath the sheet. I rub my thighs together, feeling wetness seep between my folds. Is this what it feels like to be turned on?

"Are you enjoying the view, baby?" Damon's deep voice vibrates through me, sending tingles of pleasure straight to my core.

I lift my gaze away from his large cock and find his face. His eyes are still sleepy, but the smile pulling at his full lips makes my heart skip a beat...or five. I nod my head in response to his question, afraid if I speak it will come out as a moan.

Damon's gaze darkens and his fingers trail over my body. I shiver, and my thighs spread as he moves one of his hands lazily toward my mound.

"Did checking me out turn you on? Or were you just excited to see me this morning?" His lips are at my ear. The hotness of his breath seeps into my skin. And then I feel it, the first brush of his fingers between my legs.

"I..." I stutter, my cheeks heating. I'm not really sure what I want. I want him to touch me—that I know.

"You what?" He presses his lips against my neck, and a whimper rips from deep within my chest.

"I want your fingers on me...inside me," I whisper, wondering if he even heard me. When Damon speaks again, I swear I can *hear* the smile on his face.

"Whatever you want, Keira. Whatever you want." He continues to kiss my throat and collarbone. His kisses are soft, but hold a possessiveness over me. I never thought I'd crave his touch this way, but I do. His fingers ghost against my thigh, then move lower and lower until they're at my center.

Slowly, he moves his finger against my already wet clit. The breath in my lungs slows as a knot of tension forms deep in my belly. He maintains the same rhythm until my hips start to lift off the bed and he's forced to move down.

Never removing his finger from my clit, he centers himself between my legs, spreading my thighs wide, before dipping his head closer to where I want it.

"I'm going to taste you, baby. And I want you to come on my tongue. I want to swallow every drop of your sweet cream."

Damon's words are crude, but I don't want him to stop—ever. Moans of pleasure rip through me, my belly tightening as his tongue replaces his fingers. Every lick and suck causes my body to shake with need. I'm at his mercy, and I've never been happier in my life. He continues to devour my clit, sucking hard on the little bundle of nerves.

"Oh, Damon...God..." The words rip from my throat in a haste.

An orgasm slams into me so hard, I have to close my eyes and force air into my lungs. My muscles clench hard, my pussy fluttering as if it has its own heartbeat. As I start to fall apart, I feel Damon's tongue against my pussy. It's just the tip that slips inside, but it feels amazing as he swirls it around, claiming every drop of my release as his own.

"Mmm, baby, your pussy is delectable. I'm not sure I've ever tasted such a sweet pussy before."

His admission turns me on more, and I don't understand how that's even possible. I release the grip I wasn't even aware I had on the bed sheets, and shift onto my elbows, wanting to see more of him between my legs. It's such an erotic thing to see a man between my thighs, claiming me, owning a part of me—a part I haven't even fully explored.

When one of Damon's thick fingers replaces his tongue, I tense. He lifts his eyes to mine, seeking permission or approval. The browns of my eyes must be completely gone, nearly black, but filled to the brim with desire I'm sure.

"Will it...? If I let you...is that the same as using your...?" I lick my lips and drop my gaze. I can't even say the damn word—not to him at least. A chuckle erupts from Damon's throat, and the sound startles me. I look back up at him.

Shaking his head, he keeps his gaze locked on mine. "No, Keira. Fingering you is nothing like me fucking you. You'll get pleasure from my fingers, yes, but believe me when I tell you, you'll know when my cock is inside you. And you'll beg me over and over to keep going until you fall apart."

I take a moment to relax, trusting his words, knowing when we're like this, he will never hurt me.

Leaning back, I exhale slowly. "Then please...finger me."

It's strange to say that aloud when I'm not completely certain. But I do know that I want this. I want Damon's touch. I want to feel him inside me.

"At your command, princess." His words get lost as he presses a kiss to the inside of my thigh, his hands caressing my ass while inching me forward. My heart starts beating out of my chest when I feel one of his thick fingers touch my entrance.

A low growl fills the room as Damon's finger slips inside me. It's just the tip, but it's enough to surprise and excite me all at once.

"Holy fuck, baby, you're tight as hell." He remains like this for a long moment. His heavy breathing fills my ears, and I wonder how close he is to losing control.

"Keep going, please." The words rush from my lips as his finger moves inside me painfully slow. So slow, I almost consider pleading with him to continue moving.

I mewl when his finger slips all the way in. It's not very wide or long, but it's definitely something that isn't usually there, and my body reacts to its presence. My muscles tighten, and a sting follows, but it's not so much painful as it is uncomfortable.

Just as slow, he pulls it out, then pushes it back in. His groan is audible at the sight of his finger claiming me. I wish I could see his whole face.

I go to prop myself up onto my arms again, but stop. My head falls against the pillows when he places his thumb on my clit, drawing out more moans from my lungs. The dual stimulation intensifies the feelings, and from the tightening in my pussy, it won't be long before he sends me flying over the edge all over again.

I pant, feeling each slip of his finger in and out of me. His movements are slow and purposeful, and I wonder if it always feels like this—or if it's just because it's Damon...if he's the only man who can make my body sing.

If he's able to draw this kind of pleasure from me with his fingers and his tongue, what will it be like when he fucks me for the first time? The thought scares and excites me equally. I want him bad, but I'm too terrified of the unknown to give into those needs.

The image of him pushing inside me with his long, hard pulsing dick is what drives me into oblivion.

I cry out, "Damon, Damon. Oh, God. Damon..." when the orgasm hits me full force, and he pushes his finger into me one last time while leaving his thumb on my clit, rubbing small circles against it, drawing out the sensation.

"I can't imagine what it will be like to claim you for the first time." Damon's voice is cloaked in darkness, and I know he's slightly unhinged.

As he stands, I can see the tension in his body. I want to help alleviate some of that need. I wish I knew exactly what to do on my own, but I need him to direct me.

His cock is hard, impossibly so, and if I'm being honest, it frightens me a little bit—but I don't let it stop me from reaching out for him.

Damon watches me cautiously, his body seeming to grow tenser as I grip his length. I've never held a cock in my hands before, nor brought someone to orgasm, but I want to do that for Damon. I want to make him proud. I want to make him feel the same emotions he makes me feel. My hand seems so small wrapped around him. My fingers don't even come close to meeting, and I wonder how the hell I'm supposed to do this without using two hands.

"It's taking everything inside me not to fuck the ever-loving daylights out of you, Keira. If you're planning to do something with my cock, then please do it. Otherwise, let me go, and I'll take care of it myself. I won't be liable for what happens in the next ten seconds."

His words don't sound like a threat, but there's an urgency to them, and I know he means every single word he says. If I don't do something now, he will disappear somewhere, maybe into the shower, and pleasure himself—pleasure I want to give him.

"I want to do something for you, but I don't really know how." My mind briefly wanders to when he taunted me, asking if I wanted his stripper to give me a lesson on how to please him. The memory is painful, and I shut it out as quickly as it entered.

This is just about Damon and me now.

I watch Damon visibly swallow. His body shakes as he lifts his hand, placing it over mine. His grip is harsh but warm, and I enjoy the contact of his skin against mine.

"Let me guide you," he says, exhaling a harsh breath as he moves his hand with mine over his length. His eyes peer into mine, fire flickering in his gaze, threatening to burn me alive.

His movements are slow at first, as if he's enjoying the mere contact of my hand against his cock. After a few more strokes, his hand grips mine tighter, and our pace moves together faster. Semen glistens at the edge of his cock, and my pussy quivers at the sight of it.

"Is...?" My voice shakes. "Am I doing it right?" I question, though I'm certain I am based on the sight before me. Damon's head tips back. His body is on full display, and I take the second to drink every toned inch of him in. He is a beautiful, insanely dark man, but he has a soft side, a side I want to delve into deeper.

"Fuck. Fuck yes, baby, you're doing all of it right."

I smile and continue letting him guide my hand, knowing next time I'll definitely be able to do this on my own. I peer up at him, excitement burning through me. His grip becomes harsh, and my hand starts to throb beneath his. He moves fluidly, and I become mesmerized watching the head of his cock disappear in and out of our joined hands.

"Keira..." he sighs, his body tensing, his chest heaving.

Seconds later, he comes, his seed spilling onto the sheets—well, some gets on our hands. His body shudders with aftershocks, and he relaxes his grip whiles his cock begins to soften in our hands.

I release him and gaze down at the liquid staining the sheets.

Damon grips my chin and forces my eyes to his, then he leans in. His full lips are so close, I can feel the heat of them against my own.

"I might be a fucking asshole. I might do shit that scares you, and even if I don't mean to, I may hurt you sometimes. I'm not perfect. I'm a sick and twisted man. But one thing will always remain the same—I will not let you go now. If you run, I will catch you. If you hide, I will find you. You cannot escape me. Ever. You fucking belong to me, now and forever."

His words are possessive, and I want to respond to tell him I agree. But I don't think he needs to hear me say yes. He already knows how much I need and want him.

His lips crash into mine, sealing his words with a promise.

An unsaid vow. A secret.

And that declaration almost scares me more than seeing him as the monster he claims himself to be.

10

amon

I CAN'T TAKE my eyes off her. She wasn't supposed to mean anything to me, but now she's wormed her way inside my soul inside my heart. The thought of giving her something I only gave to one other woman in my life scares me.

It terrifies me.

I loved my mother once—before I knew love was nothing more than a weakness. And all she did was turn her head, letting my father abuse my brother and I. She said she loved us. How could she not? Isn't a mother supposed to love their children by default? No matter what? If that's so, then love doesn't mean anything—or so I thought.

The scars I bare are almost unnoticeable to the naked eye, but they're a stark reminder that no one protects you from the monsters in the dark but you. No one cares for you—even if you are weak and can't care for yourself.

As I peer over at Keira in the passenger seat of my Cadillac, I'm confronted, for the first time in my life, with the idea of loving someone other than myself.

In the past, I had no one to protect me when I couldn't protect myself, but I won't let Keira suffer the same fate. I know she can't fight this alone. A battle against my brother is a losing one if she faces him alone. So I promise myself I won't let her down. I will do everything in my power to protect her. I'll give her the protection my mother failed to provide me.

When I pull into the parking lot of her old apartment complex, I see Keira's tiny body tremble.

Doesn't she know she doesn't have to be scared with me by her side?

"We're just going inside to get some of your shit, and we'll be back out to the car in a flash." I give her a calming smile, but she doesn't return one—in fact, she seems to clam up more.

"Is his body still here?" she whispers as I park and kill the engine.

"No. We disposed of it." My words are harsh, but not untrue. Typically, those who die in this business don't get a funeral. Leo was no exception.

"Like a bag of garbage? You just tossed him out." Keira shifts in her seat to face me.

I can't lie to her—nor would I even if she asked me to. I want her. I want us. And one way or another, she will have to get used to this dark and twisted life.

"Yes, Keira. In this line of work, you don't get a funeral. They draw too much attention. But don't feel bad or blame yourself. He knew what he was doing when he signed on for jobs. He knew what his fate looked like."

Keira's big brown eyes fill with tears. "I miss him, and I'm scared that when I walk back in there, all the memories will come back to me."

Her honesty shatters me. She looks like a fragile little doll— fragile enough to break, and I don't want her broken. I want her whole.

So, I comfort her in the only way I know how—with my touch. Cupping her cheek gently, I bring her face to mine, forcing her to move over the center console.

"You have nothing to fear. You have the devil on your side, and I'm willing to burn down the entire fucking town to keep you safe." My lips press against hers briefly, and when I feel her tongue probe my lips in an attempt to deepen the kiss, I pull away—even if it's the last thing I want to do. But as I told her yesterday, I can't always be the guy she wants me to be. Right now is one of those times. A tearful smile pulls at her lips, and she blinks some of them away.

"Let's get this done and over with, baby. I've got shit to do today."

We make it into the building and up to her floor before her movements start to slow. I hold her hand and tug her along, stopping once we reach the front door. I grip the handle, twisting the knob. That's strange. I remember telling Toni to lock up the place before he left. I open the door slowly, keeping Keira shielded from anyone who may already be inside the apartment.

"Wait here," I whisper, releasing her hand and crossing the threshold.

The place reeks of death, and my eyes spot the dark red splotch on the floor where she most likely found her brother. There are smatterings of blood on the walls and couch, and as I move deeper into the apartment, I can see it's been ransacked.

Fuck, Leo, what did you do to make my brother come after you? And now after your sister? I shake my head and twist on my heel, beckoning Keira forward. She's still standing in the doorway, looking every bit as afraid as she probably feels. There aren't any signs of forced entry, and the place looks...well, burglarized—but I'd expect nothing less from my brother.

"Come," I order, seeing the apprehension in her eyes. She doesn't want to, but does, her feet moving hastily over the carpet. I let her guide me into her bedroom, and I almost smile. So this is where my sweet little dove would hide from the world?

She goes straight to the closet, pulls out a suitcase, and starts shoving shit in it from the dresser. I don't think she even knows what she's taking. She's just grabbing whatever she can find. The suitcase is almost packed to the brim, and she has trouble closing it without my help. I secretly love watching her struggle, because she's cute as hell when she's flustered, but now it's nothing more than a waste of time. I'm about to give her a hand when I hear it.

The low creak of a door being opened somewhere else in the apartment.

Keira freezes beside me. I bring a finger to my lips, signaling for her to keep her mouth shut. She nods, and I reach around to grab my gun.

Slowly, and with the silence of a puma on the hunt, I make my way to the front of the apartment. As soon as I cross into the hallway, I see him.

Either he's stupid, or he didn't see me coming. The idiot stands in the middle of the room like he has no idea what the fuck is going on. His back is turned, and I use that advantage to come up behind him and hit him with the butt of my gun.

His body hits the floor with a loud thump, and I kick him in the side just for safe measure. He doesn't move. Thankfully. I don't really have the patience to deal with more shit today, but I can't pass up an interrogation session.

I eye the fucker. He looks like one of my brother's men. Dressed in a black suit, looking more like a secret agent than a fucking member of the Rossi crime family. My brother must think he's real sneaky sending people here to grab her. Like he doesn't already know what will happen if he tries to take her from me.

"Who is he?" Keira appears in the hallway, her suitcase behind her. I gaze down at her. She looks so small, so fragile. I must remind myself to be kind to her and treat her as mine.

"A soon to be dead man." I pull my phone from my pocket and dial Toni's number.

After two rings, he answers, "Boss?"

"I need some men sent out to Keira's place. I've got a live body, and I need it moved to the basement."

Keira's eyes go wide. She doesn't understand anything I've said, but she will when she sees what's going to happen.

"All right. I'll send some men out now."

On Toni's confirmation, I hang up and pocket my phone. I have half a mind to kill this bastard now, but if I do, I miss the precious opportunity to get information from him.

"Are you going to kill him?"

I shrug. "Eventually, but right now, I'm going to use him to the best of my advantage. The guy he works for is after you."

I watch as she stands in the hall nervous, her eyes refusing to look at anything but the two feet in front of her. Being here scares her, and I wish it didn't. I wish the world was a better place and she never ended up in this situation. But the world is hateful, cruel, and will kick you when you're down. And some of the scariest monsters hide in plain sight.

MY FIST CONNECTS with his jaw again, making his head swing to the side. Blood pours from his nose and mouth. My knuckles start to swell and turn blue. The pain is an absent thought—I could do this all night, but beating the shit out of him with my fists isn't going to get me the answers I want.

I decide to switch to a knife to get this show on the road. As soon as I unsheathe the blade the bastard's eyes go wide.

"Are you ready to tell me why my brother sent you? Or maybe what the fuck he wants with Keira?" I loom over him, sliding the blade across the fucker's bare chest. He has a Rossi Crime tattoo on his chest, and I consider skinning him and sending the fucking thing to my brother.

"I'm a dead man anyway, but you know that already—so why would I tell you anything?" He can barely talk. Blood is filling his mouth from a cut inside his cheek, and he keeps spitting the red out. It flies everywhere, and it's fucking annoying the shit out of me.

"You are right about that, but if you do tell me what I want to know I'll kill you much quicker and with much less pain. Maybe if you tell me now, I won't come after the people you love next." The asshole starts laughing, actually fucking laughing, and I wonder if this guy has balls of steel.

"You know better than anyone that guys like us don't get to love anybody. No family. No kids. No wives. You can try to kill 'em but they don't exist."

I know we shouldn't have attachments.

I walk over to the table and select a new knife, a deadlier one. I run my thumb over the sharp edge. The blade cuts into my skin, causing the blood to swell over the insignificant cut.

Sharp enough to cut through bone...I hope. I rub at my jaw, staring down at the idiot like he's a science project instead of a human.

"Alright then, let's see if you change your mind after I carve some holes in your legs." With complete precision, I take the knife and start cutting slowly into his upper thigh. I take my time slicing through skin as if I'm field dressing an animal. The fucker starts screaming right away. Music to my fucking ears.

I would be a lying bastard if I said his screams didn't bring me immense pleasure. Having this kind of control and power makes me feel invincible—like a fucking king. I toss the chunk of flesh to the floor like it's a piece of garbage. Blood is everywhere—on my hands, dripping on the floor.

I'm about to slice a second piece of flesh out when the door opens.

I look up from the task at hand, ready to yell at the unlucky bastard who walked in at the wrong time when I realize it isn't one of my men—but my woman. Beautiful, vibrant brown eyes stare back at me, and for a moment, they make me stop and forget where I am and what I'm doing.

"I told you to wait upstairs," I snarl.

I don't like her seeing this side of me—the darker, unhinged side. I want to be a good man and hide and shield all the bad in the world from her.

"I don't want you to kill him." Her voice is small and pleading, and that makes me furious.

Doesn't she understand how this works?

"You do realize he would have killed you in a heartbeat. Actually, he would have probably raped you first, then killed you."

I watch her recoil at my words, and I almost wish I wouldn't have said them, but she needs to hear this. Needs to understand what kind of people are after her. They're not like me. They will not offer her a chance. They'll just take. Which is why I'm here now, protecting her, making certain she's okay.

"Why don't you stay and watch?"

Her eyes go wide, but she doesn't make a move to leave. Her body trembles, and I fear how she'll look at me after this moment.

Shoving the insecure thoughts away, I turn my attention back to the asshole in front of me. "Last chance to speak."

"Fuck you," he gurgles.

I'm shocked the man hasn't bled out yet. Must be his lucky day.

"Nice choice of final words." I grab him by the head and pull it back, exposing his throat. I hold the knife to the skin under his ear and drag it across to the other side. The knife easily slides through the flesh.

If he wasn't bleeding out before—he is now. Blood pours from the wound like a small waterfall over his chest and into his lap. There's a copper tinge to the air, and I can taste blood on my tongue.

My gaze flashes to Kiera standing in the doorway, looking like she grew roots and became one with the floor. I place the knife back on the table and take a step toward her. All the blood drains from her face, making her look as pale as a ghost. I'm not doing this to scare her, but to show her how ruthless this world can be—and maybe so she can see the real monster I am.

"This is how my world works, Keira. It has been like this since before I was born, and it's never going to change. It's kill or be killed."

Shock and fear reflect back at me in her eyes, giving away just how terrified she is. I want to comfort her, but my hand and clothes still have this fucker's blood on them.

I can't touch her like this. I don't think she would want me to touch her either. I take another step toward her, and she takes a step back. Then she stares at me for a long moment before turning and running back the way she came.

Emotions swirl out of control inside me. Maybe giving her some time to digest this would be the best plan of action—because as badly as I want to go to comfort her, I know she needs to see this for what it is.

A world where you kill or be killed.

eira

WITNESSING Damon as the cruel criminal he's always claimed to be is terrifying. I knew he killed people, but there's nothing like actually seeing it occur right in front of you. I walk up the stairs two at a time and right past two of his men standing guard at the top.

They don't pay me any attention, and I don't pay them any. I'm confused. My stomach twists into knots. The same hands that bring me pleasure, also deliver death.

I need to stop thinking about that man in the basement, imagining him dead. I start walking around the club carelessly. I don't want to be here right now, but I told Damon I wouldn't leave again, and I wasn't going to break that promise—no matter what he had done.

Instead of breaking down crying or running away, I head back to Damon's office. The hall is quiet, quieter than usual. I'm almost to the door, my fingers grasping for the knob, but that's as far as I get.

In an instant, someone grabs me from behind, flipping me around and slamming me into the nearest wall. My vision blurs. The air in my lungs expels. Fear overtakes me.

Before a scream can rip from my throat, a hand is wrapping around it, squeezing so hard, blackness overtakes my vision.

Eyes so dark and cold they make me shiver stare me down. I've never seen this man's face before, but he looks oddly familiar.

"Sweet, Kiera, I've been looking for you."

He smells dangerous, and his body takes up all the space in the hall. He holds me with little effort, and I don't even make an attempt to escape. There would be no point. He could easily snap my neck.

"Didn't you get my message? I told you I was coming for you. You should have just waited for me at your place." There's a hint of humor to his words. A sinister smile pulls at his lips, revealing perfectly straight white teeth. Of course, the lion about to devour me has perfect teeth.

He leans closer, his nose skimming over my throbbing pulse. "I hope my brother has taken good care of you for me."

Brother?

He must see the confusion and shock in my eyes. He pulls back a little and releases his grip on my throat. I suck in a greedy breath.

"Damon didn't tell you, did he? That you belong to his big brother."

The man before me picks up a piece of hair off my shoulder. His eyes inspect it like it's the most beautiful thing he's ever seen.

"You know the only reason he wants you is because I own you. He always wants things that don't belong to him. He's been that way since we were kids."

I know I need to try and remain calm, to use my voice, to make myself heard.

"No one owns me, not you, and definitely not Damon." The man smirks at me, and in his eyes, I see pain and death.

"Is that so?" His words tickle my ear, and before I know it, I'm being dragged through the back door. I'm just about to ask a question when the door to an SUV opens and the man holding my arm pushes me inside. "Let's go for a ride, Keira. I have a couple questions to ask you about your brother."

I gulp as his big body climbs in behind me. I move across the bench seat, going to the other side of the car, huddling near the door.

When the door to the SUV closes, trapping me inside with this nameless man, I panic. My body starts to shake, and black dots appear over my vision.

"Relax. I'm not going to kill you." He smiles, then adds, "Yet."

"I don't have anything, and I know nothing. I swear." Tears sting my eyes. A part of me feels like life would be easier if I died. All I'm doing now is running from one monster to another.

When the SUV starts moving, I sink my fingers into the leather seat, wishing I could go back in time.

"I'm sorry for not introducing myself sooner. I'm Xander Rossi."

I blink, my eyes lifting to his. Now I understand why his face looked so familiar. He's an older looking version of Damon. Everything he said now makes sense.

"You're Damon's brother," I whisper.

He chuckles. "I see you've finally put the pieces together." The man before me screams danger and oozes power. It's a scary combination.

"You're the one after me, so what do you want?" I already know the answer.

He stares at me a moment. There is no warmth in his brown eyes, no emotions, nothing.

"*That. I. Am.* I have some questions for you, and as long as you answer them to the best of your knowledge, nothing ill will happen to you. But lie to me, Keira..." His hand lifts and comes to rest against my knee. He gently squeezes it, a warning, proving the hold he has over me.

I shiver. Fear like I've never felt spirals out of control inside me. "Please don't," I whimper.

"I won't hurt you...not unless I have to. You're more valuable alive than dead, but that doesn't mean I won't hurt you if you lie to me."

I nod. All I need to do is answer his questions, and then I can walk away.

"What...? What do you want to know?" I stumble, feeling small and insignificant in his presence.

"Well, first..." He releases his hold on my knee and casually leans back, "were you aware your brother was stealing money from me?"

I shake my head. I get the feeling I'm not going to like the things I discover about my brother today.

"Use words," Xander demands.

"No. I didn't know." I gain enough courage to spit the words out, knowing if I didn't, I could end up with a black eye. Xander doesn't look like he's opposed to beating women, and I don't really want to find out.

"Good. So, you're telling me you had no idea your brother was doing illegal things? Drug trafficking, auctions, prostitution."

I blink, the contents of my stomach churning. Now I know why my brother always had money—why he was able to afford clothes and my schooling.

"I didn't know. I knew he was making good money, but I didn't know what he was doing. He never shared his work with me—and I never asked."

Xander stares at me, appearing to digest my response. I lick my lips, afraid he may not accept my answer and I'll end up dead on the side of the road in a gutter—or worse, raped and beaten.

"I swear..." I whimper, feeling Xander's cold gaze on my face. Time seems to stand still.

"Do you know what is going to happen to you if you lie to me, or try to run from me again?"

I shake my head. "N-N-o-o."

Xander smiles, leaning his body into mine, causing me to curl into myself. "If I find you've done either of those things, I will hunt you down and take you back to my club, then I will fuck you bloody until you beg me to stop. And when I've had my fill, I'll give you to my men to be used. They'll fuck you as well, and then they'll slit your throat and watch the blood drain from your lifeless body."

The SUV comes to a stop, and without thinking, I open the passenger door. All the contents in my stomach empty onto the ground. My eyes burn, tears slipping down my cheeks. I feel a cold gun pressed into my side, halting any further movement.

My body shakes with every breath I take. My brother got himself killed gaining an easy way out, but I'm still alive, and I'm paying for his actions.

"Do you understand the consequences, Keira?" I feel his hot breath on my neck. I'm still hanging out the side of the car, my body swaying like leaves in the breeze.

"Yes. Yes, I understand." The words come out calm, too calm, and I wonder how long it'll be before death and I meet.

I'm alone, tired, exhausted, and above all, I am done.

"Good. Get the fuck out of my car. I'll be back to check on you, and when I do, you better be here." Xander gives me a shove, and I slip out of the SUV on wobbly legs.

"Oh, and don't tell Damon about our little conversation. This one stays between you and I, sweetheart."

My knees go weak, and I almost fall to the ground. Then he closes the door behind him, and the SUV drives off into the night, as if it was never there to begin with.

I'm back in Night Shift's parking lot. The evil cycle continues. I'm trapped between the Rossi brothers.

With the bright street lights shining down on me, I move into the packed parking lot. I'm not sure where I'm going or what I'm going to do. I doubt my bank cards work anymore, and even if I did run away, Damon and Xander would come for me. They both threatened me, and I believe them.

I have no place to go. No place to hide. No way out of this.

There's only one thing to do.

A choice must be made.

And it will be the lesser evil.

I drag my feet across the parking lot, forcing each step toward the back door. Before I can even lift my hand to reach for the handle, the door flies open and Damon's large frame appears in front of me. His eyes are full of fury, like a bull on the verge of charging—at me.

"What the hell are you doing out here?"

I want to tell him what happened—that I know his brother is the man after me. I want Damon to take me in his arms and tell me everything is going to be okay...tell me he will always protect me —even from his own brother. But Xander's warning rings in my ears, and I can't shake the threat. He might not kill Damon, but he'll kill me, and I value my life—even if it is pretty shitty right now.

"I just needed some fresh air," I lie, trying to hide the tiredness and sadness from my face. I'm starting to think the only way out of this mess will be from a bullet to the head.

The fury rolling off Damon pulls me back to the present. His anger suffocates me, and I hate that he's mad and there's nothing I can do about it.

He doesn't buy what I've told him, and I think he can smell the lie on me.

Instead of dragging me back inside—like I half expected—he walks outside, letting the door close behind him.

"Let's go home." He unlocks his car and grabs my hand, tugging me along. I can still feel the anger radiating off him, but he does a better job concealing it now. It isn't until we are in the car that I notice Damon is clean and wearing different clothes. I guess he keeps extra clothes on hand for when things get messy.

I get into the car and lean against the window.

I'm caught between two killers.

One wants to love me, and one wants to literally kill me.

The chances of surviving this horrible predicament seem slimmer and slimmer everyday...and still...when I close my eyes, I see myself with Damon, celebrating a life I know we will never be able to live.

A life full of love and laughter—full of happiness.

amon

I DON'T WANT to lose it, but I feel the blackness closing around me. This is why feelings never work. Why I promised myself I would never fall for a woman.

My thoughts are twisted and warped, mixing with my past. I know I need to care for Keira, but she makes it so fucking hard when she doesn't listen—when she's so naive and kind. It literally kills me to bring her into the darkness.

She rests against the passenger window. Her eyes are closed, and she looks as if she is sleeping. I grip the steering wheel, trying to cool my heated blood, trying to stop myself from losing it.

I keep the fury contained long enough to make it home, and as soon as I park and get out, I lose it. I unleash myself against the brick exterior of the house. My fists slam into the unforgiving brick over and over. The pain reminds me I am in fact human, and very capable of breaking bones.

Blood starts dripping down my fists, but I don't stop until I've taken the edge off the top and first layer of skin of my knuckles. My chest heaves as I suck precious oxygen into my lungs. I turn around and see Keira waiting for me. Her eyes are sad, dull, and I wish like hell they were sparkling with excitement or desire— hell, even fear would be a better emotion than the one I am seeing right now.

"Why did you lie to me?"

She averts her gaze, and the gesture gives her away, confirming she lied.

When she doesn't answer, I start up the front steps and open the door, swinging it wide. She follows behind like a meek little mouse. I slam the door shut, then turn on her—right as she's taking her shoes off.

"Were you planning to run again? I thought we were past that, Keira. I thought you wanted my protection?"

Tears well in her eyes, threatening to spill over and down her cheeks.

"I..." she croaks, her voice full of unknown emotion.

"You what? You thought it'd be better? Easier to run from your problems?" I squeeze my lids shut, frustration and anger coursing through my veins, threatening to break through to the surface. I run my fingers through my hair, pulling hard against the strands. I take a step toward Keira and watch as she retreats a step.

"Is that what you were doing? Running? Did you think you could get away from me again?" I close the space between us in a second. My hands grip her hips with a bruising touch, and I stare straight into her brown eyes.

"I'd never run from you, Damon. Not again."

My eyes trail over her beautiful face, her tired eyes, and down over her body. The air around us sizzles as soon as my eyes land on her throat.

The faint bruises on her creamy white skin stick out like a sore thumb. I lift my eyes to her face and see fear rattling around inside her. She's scared shitless, and I doubt I'll get an answer out of her about who did this—even if I ask.

The sound of my phone ringing in my pocket angers me. I don't want to answer right now. I just want to make Keira tell me who the fuck I need to kill. I grab my phone anyway, nearly breaking the fucking thing when I see the name flash across the screen.

I lift my gaze to Keira once more—fresh tears have fallen on her cheeks, and I don't know how she still has more tears inside her. Suddenly, everything falls into place, and I make the connection. The reason why she would lie to me...why she is so fucking afraid right now... why there are bruises around her neck—like someone was choking her.

"He did this, didn't he? Xander. He put his fucking hands on you."

Keira's wide-eyed expression confirms my assumption.

I'm unsure how the bastard got into the club without anyone knowing, but it's clear he planted that bastard in her apartment to distract me. Or maybe he didn't, and I was just too fucking concerned with killing some fucker instead of protecting her. Either way, I feel like a pile of shit for not being there for her.

Pulling Keira into my arms, I press soft kisses against her throat, over the bruises my piece of shit brother left on her skin.

"I will kill him for this, Keira. I will kill him," I whisper against her flesh, and she sobs into my chest.

"He told me not to say anything," she mutters. "Why didn't you tell me he was your brother?"

I can feel the fragile trust blooming between us wither away.

"Xander and I might share some blood, but I don't consider him my brother. I didn't tell you because I didn't think it mattered. It doesn't change anything. I'll kill him for hurting you."

Some of the tension disappears from her body as she relaxes into my touch—as if she knows this is where she belongs. I bend down to pick her up, and her arms snake around my neck and her legs wrap around my midsection, holding on to me tightly. I can feel her warmth seep into me.

I carry her down the hall and into my bedroom, placing her gently on my bed.

"I'm going to call back Xander."

I use the seconds it takes to pull my phone out and dial his number to compose myself—to the best of my ability.

I want nothing more than to scream all the ways I plan on killing him, but I know that would be a bad move...so I rein in my fury for a moment. Taking a deep, calming breath, I wait for him to answer.

It rings, and ring, then his asshole voice filters through the phone speaker.

"Damon, I've been trying to reach you. I even came by the club once, but I seem to keep missing you."

I clench my fist. This fucker thinks he's sneaky. Has he forgotten I know him—far more than anyone else? That he can't fool me?

"What do you want, Xander?"

He chuckles. "I can't simply call you and have a conversation? I do miss you little brother. It's probably time we catch up."

"Don't pretend you have any emotions, Xander. We both know better, and I'd much rather discuss this over the phone...so just tell me what you want."

"This isn't something we can discuss over the phone. I'm afraid I'll need to see you and Keira in the flesh. So please don't make this a hassle, dear ol' brother. Meet me tomorrow at the Rossi Mansion. I assume you still know where that is?"

"Yes, we'll be there. And, Xander, if you ever lay a finger on my property again, I will gut you like a fish," I growl and hang up the phone, trying to forget my fucking brother and think about nothing besides the goddess lying in my bed.

There's no saying what will happen tomorrow—or what my brother will do to her...or me. I've seen his darkness, tasted it even, but I don't want Keira to see it.

I'm distracted from my thoughts when she sits up, her eyes boring into mine. She looks at me like she wants to say something but instead she stands in front of me. Grabbing the hem of her shirt, she pulls it over her head. Then she reaches behind and undoes her bra. I'm so mesmerized that I just stand there and watch her. Her nice perky tits are free now, and her nipples are pointing at me.

I've seen a lot of girls take their clothes off. I own a fucking strip club for God's sake. But this has to be the sexiest fucking striptease I've ever seen. Her eyes never leave mine. She is completely fixated on me while she slowly undoes her pants and pulls them down, taking her panties with them.

"I want you tonight. I want you to fuck me," she mutters, standing in front of me completely naked now.

"Who knows what's going to happen tomorrow. It's not set in stone, and after everything, I don't want to waste any more time."

Everything she says is true, but that doesn't mean I want to admit it.

"I'll protect you tomorrow and any other fucking day of the year. That's what's going to happen. As for the future, we'll take it one step at a time."

I keep a small amount of distance between us, afraid that if I get too close, I'll swallow her whole. She's mouthwatering, and I want to possess her, own her, but not under these circumstances. I don't want her to do this because she is scared.

"I don't care. I still want you. I want it to be you." She takes a step toward me and starts unbuttoning my shirt.

Her hands are a little shaky, but she has a smile on her face. She is nervous, but not scared of me. She knows I won't hurt her. Still, I feel the need to say it out loud.

"We'll go slow. I'll try not to hurt you, and if you ever want me to stop, just say the words and I will." I push a few strands of hair from her face as she gets done unbuttoning my shirt. She shoves it off my shoulders and lets it fall to the floor.

"But know we don't have to do this. We don't have to do anything today."

Her cheeks a soft pink, and her eyes filled with arousal and excitement, she whispers, "Shut up and kiss me."

I'm not used to following commands, but I am willing to make an exception today, and I obey. Leaning down, I press my lips to hers. She is close enough now that her pebbled nipples rub against my bare chest. There is no other feeling like her body against mine. My cock springs to life in response—so ready to finally be inside her.

It's caught between us, pressing firmly against her flat belly. I nip at her lips, urging her to open to me. When she does, my tongue slips inside, swirling around her mouth, mingling with her tongue, tasting her.

I kiss her like that for a long time, tasting her, trailing my fingers up and down her arms. I want this to be perfect for her. I might not be able to save her from all the bad in this world, but I can give her this moment. I can make certain it's all she ever thought it would be.

When I finally pull away, Keira is breathless. Her eyes peer up at me with adoration. I can see she feels safe in my arms, and I never want that to change. With a soft smile, I ease her onto the bed, watching her face as I do.

"I'm going to make this good for you—so fucking good for you, baby," I whisper against her skin, peppering kisses over her throat, collarbone, and chest. Anger flickers inside me as I notice the bruises again, then I move my lips lower.

I take one of her hard nipples into my mouth, swirling my tongue around the tip, and she arches her back off the bed. Her hands make their way into my hair, holding my face against her tit.

I wonder if I could make her fall apart with nothing more than my tongue on her nipple. I smile against her skin, saving it for another day. When I release her tit with a pop, I knead her other breast, rolling the nipple between two fingers, giving them equal attention.

By the time I pull my hands away, she's panting, her eyes are dilated, and I'd bet anything if I dipped my finger inside her she'd be wet as the fucking ocean.

Stripped of my shirt already, I shuck my pants and boxers in one swoop and drop down to my knees, gripping Keira by the ankles and pulling her ass to the very edge of the mattress.

Propping herself up on her elbows, she licks her lips and eyes me, looking like a vixen.

"You going to watch me devour your pussy?" I growl, a possessiveness overtaking me. She belongs to me.

Mine.

The word vibrates inside my head, but I don't think about what it means.

Without warning, I dive between her legs like a starved man. My fingers sink into her smooth flesh, and she lifts her hips with every lick of my tongue—as if she knows exactly what she fucking needs.

"Damon..." she gasps, her head falling back against the mattress. I smirk against her perfect pink pussy and grip her ass, lifting her hips upward, alternating between long licks and sucking on her little clit.

It doesn't take long for her to start thrashing against the sheets. Pants and moans escape her lips, but I keep up my relentless pace until she falls off the fucking edge. Her pussy quivers, and her delicious sweet cream coats my tongue.

Her legs are still shaking, and her eyes are squeezed closed when I press a finger against her soaked entrance. The thick digit enters her easily. Fuck, how I wish it was my cock claiming her right now and not my finger.

I take a couple calming breaths, reminding myself it will be worth it.

Soon...so fucking soon.

I need her panting, soaked to the bone, and primed for my cock.

"You're so beautiful when you come." I nudge her legs wide and slowly insert a second finger, scissoring them. She mewls, placing her arm over her mouth—as if she's worried the whole neighborhood may hear.

"Be loud, baby. Scream if necessary. Tell everyone how much you love the things I do to your body." I want to hear her. I want to watch her face as she falls apart again and again. I want to swallow every last drop of her cum.

Using my thumb, I rub fast circles against her clit, all while moving two fingers in and out of her tight hole. My cock throbs, and all the blood in my body roars to life, beckoning me to take her. I push the need down and continue fingering her, bringing her closer and closer to oblivion with each stroke. Only a few more moments pass, and she's coming again. Her orgasm drips down my hand as her pussy tightens around my fingers, damn near squeezing the life out of them.

My own chest heaves, and when I ease my fingers out, I bring them to my lips and taste her sweetness one last time before I move above her.

Keira opens her eyes. The brown is brighter than I've ever seen it. Need and desire shine in her eyes. The look she wears gives me confirmation that she wants me, and I know she is ready now.

Her pussy is slick, prepared to accommodate my cock.

I move her back up the bed, making sure there's enough space to climb on top of her. She watches every move I make like a hawk. Fear and nervousness is absent. There is only excitement and anticipation in her eyes—as if the moment can't happen fast enough for her...when I want the damn moment to last forever.

With my entire body hovering inches from hers, I feel an electric charge between us. An invisible force is begging us to join, pulling our bodies together like we are magnetic.

"I'll be as gentle as I can. If at any time you want me to stop, you tell me...okay?" I take her by the chin, making certain she hears every word.

When I release my hold, she nods. "I won't stop you, Damon. I want you. I want this. I want it so badly, it hurts."

Her words slam into my heart, ripping off the Band-Aid from a wound that never healed. She needs me. She wants this...wants me. And I can't say I've ever had a woman want me for the unapologetic bastard I am.

As I fist my cock in my hand, I stare deep into her eyes, knowing love truly is an incredible emotion.

And I'm pretty fucking close to feeling it.

eira

HE LOOKS at me like he wants to consume and cherish me all at once. I can feel how much he wants me...wants this moment between us. And I wish like hell that I could stop time just for us —so we can enjoy this moment again and again.

Damon's body shakes as if it's taking an extreme amount of effort not to slam inside me. It feels like we've been waiting to do this forever—which is ridiculous. I only met Damon days ago. How is it possible I feel so strongly? It feels like he knows me better than anyone.

I think the most important thing is that I feel like I'm the only one who knows him—the real him...the man beneath the mask he slips on every day. He shows bits and pieces of the person he really is. The man he thrives to be.

Pressing between my legs, he exhales a shaky breath. He looks on edge—like if I reach out and touch him, he might cut me. But it's a risk I'm willing to take. I'll travel into the dark with him if it means he comes out a better man.

He leans down, keeping most of his weight on one arm. The feel of his body on mine leaves me panting with need. He kisses me again. His lips are possessive and heated and I want to take my hand and hold his lips to mine, but I also want him to slip inside me.

I moan into his mouth, begging him to take me. I can feel him guiding himself to my wet slit, and I lift my hips to meet his touch. The silky, smooth head of his thick cock is right at my entrance, and I shudder remembering how he made me come like this yesterday.

My hands snake around his huge body, my fingers digging into his shoulder, urging him to come closer. His skin is so soft and warm beneath my touch. I don't want an inch of space between us. Even the air separating us feels like too much.

Damon swoops down, pressing his lips against mine. He kisses me deeply, taking my mouth like a starved man. I melt farther into the mattress, my softness rubbing against all his hard edges. He ends the kiss and places his forehead against mine.

We're both panting. Desire pools deep in his eyes, and he hitches my leg up, guiding his cock straight toward my pussy. He enters me slowly, his body quivering as he exhales a calming breath.

"Keira," he pants. "You feel like heaven."

I can see how much he wants me—how much he wants this. Swiveling his hips, he moves a couple more inches inside.

My body stretches farther to accommodate his huge cock, and I gasp slightly, my chest constricting from the fullness. I've never felt anything like this before. I suck my bottom lip into my mouth to stifle a whimper.

Will he be able to fit?

Damon shifts his head and places it in the crook of my neck. I can hear him inhale as if he's trying calm himself.

"Fuck, Keira, you're so tight," Damon whispers against my hair as he works himself deeper inside me—until I feel him at the back of my channel. As soon as he's fully seated, he stills, allowing me to adjust to his length.

There's a slight burning and an overwhelming fullness consuming me, but there is far less pain than I ever expected.

"Baby," he hisses. "I've got to start moving soon."

I can tell he's barely holding on. I feel the need pulsing through him.

"I'm okay...move. It doesn't hurt. I just feel full." My voice comes out as nothing more than a breath.

A deep growl that sounds more animal than human rips from Damon's throat, and holy hell, he finally starts to move.

He thrust his hips slowly, pulling out of me before easing back in, setting a wonderful rhythm that has me panting. Warmth tingles down my spine. It's different than the kind of pleasure he's given me with his tongue and fingers.

This is a deeper pleasure. Soul searing, body consuming.

Damon does this for a short time, his hips flexing just enough for me to feel him deeper than previously. Each movement gives me unbelievable pleasure. Feeling the pressure build deep in my core, I tighten my legs around his middle, my feet digging into his ass, pulling him closer. My body is scorching hot as he peppers open mouthed kisses around my jawline until he reaches my ear.

"You'll always be mine now," he whispers possessively before nipping on my earlobe, and I know he means that. I'll always be his, and in return, he will always be mine.

An electric current flows through my veins as his body claims mine with each thrust and kiss. I can feel how close I am to coming, the orgasm building deep within.

"Come for me, baby. Milk my cock. Squeeze it tight. Give me your first of many orgasms on my cock."

His hard length seems to grow as he throbs inside me. My skin burns everywhere he touches, but his words are what drive me over the edge into pure bliss.

As if he has a direct line to my pussy, my body follows his command and my walls clench around him as a mind blowing orgasm hits me. The feeling is so overwhelming, for a moment, I don't know where I am or what's going on. All I feel is pleasure consuming my every thought. Completely disoriented, I hold onto Damon, clinging to his body as I try to catch my breath.

Damon grinds his pelvis into my center. The sensation is so deep, my toes curl against his backside. He does this a few more times before I feel his body shudder against mine. His jaw goes slack, and his eyes drift closed. He grunts, and I feel a warmth in my womb as he releases his hot seed. Remaining seated inside me, he hovers above me, and the closeness of his body makes me feel safe.

Sex, sweat, and our unique scents coat the air. I realize now I wouldn't care if I smelled Damon's scent on me for the rest of my life. It all makes me feel safe—safer than I've felt in a long time.

After a short while, when his cock finally goes soft inside me, Damon pulls out, rolling over onto his side, taking me and the blanket with him. Tucking me into his chest, I cuddle as close as I can to him.

"I love you," I mumble against his chest, then panic rips through me. I'm not sure if he heard me, and he doesn't say anything back.

I don't think a man like him is very familiar with the word, let alone the concept of it.

"You don't have to say it back. I just wanted to tell you before tomorrow. I don't know what's going to happen, and I want you to know you mean more to me than you think."

Silence blankets us. I snuggle deeper into his chest, praying even after tomorrow, we will get another chance to do this.

My eyes drift shut, and it's then I hear his words.

"I don't know if I'm capable of loving at all. Not anymore. Not after my past. But if I could love someone, it would be you. It would be you."

My chest constricts, and I know we need to survive tomorrow—we need to survive Xander. Not only to live, but maybe also to love.

I WAKE up in the cocoon that is Damon. His arms are slung around me, and one of his legs is draped across both of mine, securing me to his body, making certain I don't escape. I have just enough room to breathe, and as my skin moves against his, I realize how sticky and hot we both are.

Memories of the night before flood my mind. The way he cared for me and brought my body to unforeseen heights. I never expected him to be so gentle.

I peer at Damon's sleeping form. He looks so at peace, so happy, and I wish he could remain like this forever.

I wish we could run away together and leave this life behind.

Emotions swarm me as I realize today I'll be forced to see Xander again—the man who had my brother killed. Damon said he would protect me, but can he? Can he protect me from his own brother?

Leo paid in blood...and for what? Stealing money? I didn't realize I was crying until I felt wetness against my cheeks. Pushing my face against Damon's chest, I try to stop myself from letting any more tears fall. He stirs next to me, pulling me tighter into his embrace—almost squeezing me so hard, I can't breathe.

When a wheezing noise escapes me, he pulls my face toward his and stares into my eyes.

"Are you okay?"

"Yeah. I think sometimes you forget how strong you are."

"Were you crying?"

"I was just thinking about my brother...that's all."

"I'm sorry." He takes my face between his two large hands, wiping the tears away with his thumbs.

"Everything is going to be okay. I can't bring back your brother, but I can make sure nothing happens to you."

He kisses my cheeks, then claims my mouth. I can still taste the salty wetness on his lips. Deepening the kiss, I pull him closer, moaning into his mouth. Maybe I can trust Damon. Maybe I can believe everything will be okay.

Damon breaks the kiss before it turns into something more, leaving me panting with need. "I don't think you know what you're asking for, baby."

I can feel his hardening cock against my leg, and I want to tell him I know exactly what I'm asking for, but Damon continues talking.

"I'd love nothing more than to take your begging pussy, but you need a break after last night. So how about we go get some breakfast before I change my mind—because I can guarantee you wouldn't want me to take you again right now."

I nibble on my bottom lip mischievously. "And why is that? You don't know what I want?"

Damon smirks. A predatory look fixes his eyes. "I did everything I could last night to make your first time everything you could have ever wanted, but right now, I want to fuck you like an animal in heat."

I shiver, but I'm positive it's not from fear—not when the muscles in my belly tighten.

"The idea is intriguing, but I can't control myself right now— and I won't hurt you. So get your beautiful ass out of bed and help me make breakfast."

My brow furrows. "You cook?"

Damon untangles himself from my body and climbs out of bed.

"I don't like having people in my house. I have someone who cleans once a week, but that's it—and usually, I'm here when she is. But I don't want staff around, and I don't want to eat take-out every night. That's left me with one single option: cook for myself."

It dawns on me what this house means to Damon and why he's so different here compared to how he is at the club—or anywhere else.

This place is his sanctuary. It's the only place he can be himself. The only place he doesn't have to pretend to be anything else. He doesn't have to be a hardened criminal here because there's no one to answer to.

"So, you don't like having me in your house?" I ask playfully.

"You're the exception to any and all my rules—not that it would matter anyway. This place is as much your home as it is mine. Now, come put some clothes on. My self-control is withering away as we speak."

I smile, loving that I have some kind of hold over him. He wants to protect me. He wants me safe and unharmed, and that makes my heart beat faster inside my chest.

I watch him get dressed, my gaze greedily taking in his every movement. As soon as I stand, I feel the tenderness between my legs. My thighs are sticky, and I turn around noticing a smattering of blood against the sheets.

Damon's gaze moves from my face to the bed sheets, and I know he's watching me piece the puzzle together.

"Blood is normal after the first time. It's nothing to be scared of, and there shouldn't be any next time. It wasn't from me taking you too roughly, because I can assure you I didn't take you as hard as I could have—nor as hard as I wanted to."

My cheeks heat at the thought. My body burning up, and my insides tingling with desire.

"I know you didn't, and I know you were holding back."

Damon's jaw clenches in a way that makes me think he might be mad. Does he think he's weak for being so kind to me? Or maybe he's worried I thought he acted like a savage. But didn't I? I thought he'd take me as he had all the other women he'd been with.

"I'm sorry if I offended you. I didn't mean it like that. I just know you were trying to be kind—that you didn't want to hurt me." I'm digging a deeper hole.

When Damon doesn't say anything, I decide to shut up and take a shower.

"I think I'm going to take a quick shower before I get dressed."

I feel awkward now, and I hate it. I ruined a good morning all because I couldn't keep my damn mouth shut.

Feeling shameful, I start toward the bathroom when a hand on my shoulder halts my movements. Damon's grip tightens as he turns me into his chest. Two fingers bring my chin upward, and I'm forced to look at him.

"It's okay to see me as the monster I am, Keira, but it's not okay to assume I would ever hurt you. I care for you like I've never cared for anyone, and just because I fuck like a beast doesn't mean I'd take you that way. I can control myself. I can put the monster away to give you a piece of my heart."

I don't even realize I have tears in my eyes until I feel the damn things sliding down my cheeks. I nod, pressing up on my tiptoes to kiss him. He lets me, but only briefly. Then he releases me, his eyes blazing with need.

"Go...now," he growls, then turns around and walks out of the room, disappearing down the hallway.

I stand there a moment longer, my feet cemented into the floor before I make my way into his bathroom. It's huge, magnificent, and has a fancy shower with multiple steam functions. It reminds me of those luxury showers you see in commercials or movies. I check out all the settings and decide that a nice steamy shower is exactly what I need. Turning the knob all the way to hot, I get in and let the water massage and heat my tender flesh. I always tense up when I get stressed out, and it makes my neck stiff and sore. The past few days have been stressful as hell and you better believe my neck is letting me know it.

I stand under the shower way longer than I intended, so by the time I get out, my skin resembles a prune. Feeling ten times less stressed and a hundred times refreshed, I wrap myself up in a fluffy towel. Glad to have a bigger selection of clothes here now, I grab some fresh underwear, an *ACDC* shirt that used to be my brother's, and a pair of skinny jeans. I dress quickly, brush my teeth, and comb through a dark mop of russet-brown hair.

Once I have the rat's nest tamed, I make my way to the kitchen, letting my nose guide me the entire way. There's a delicious scent filling the air, and I'm half shocked Damon wasn't lying about his cooking skills.

As soon as I round the corner and step into the kitchen, I realize I must have spent way more time in the shower than I thought. Damon has already finished cooking and is setting the table.

"Quick shower, huh?" He snickers.

"Sorry," I mutter, giving him a shy smile. I feel bad about the fact that he had to make breakfast all alone, but a few extra minutes in the shower was completely worth it.

"It's fine. Sit. Eat. You'll need to replenish if you plan on doing anything else today." He winks and points to a chair as he sets a plate down. A good portion of eggs topped with veggies and bacon cover it. I do as he asks, inhaling the aroma of the food.

My gaze lifts to Damon's. He looks at home, appearing as if this all comes natural. And with every new thing I learn about him, I want to learn more. There isn't enough time in the day to learn what makes him tick.

I lift my fork and dig in. It's hot as hell and nearly burns my tongue, but the flavor explodes in my mouth—the taste even better than it smells. The veggies are cooked perfectly, and the eggs are fluffy and mixed with a little bit of cheese.

"Wow, this is really good."

"Now, if you would say that with a little less surprise, I might actually take it as a compliment." He laughs a belly-shaking chuckle.

I'm slightly shocked, and I hope he can't tell. I want to hear that kind of happiness escape his lips again. I take a drink of orange juice, then swallow down the food in my mouth.

His deep laugh echoes throughout the large kitchen. It's infectious. And I start laughing. I've never seen Damon so at ease, and it makes me happy and less nervous. Our carefree morning routine comes to a halt though when his cell phone rings. His eyes gloss, and all happiness drains from his face. The mask I often see him wear slips back into place.

He lets the call go to voicemail, then the phone chimes again.

I try to focus on finishing my breakfast and less on what he is doing, but my appetite is gone now.

"It's Xander, and he wants us to come to dinner. He's also invited the rest of our family."

My brows pinch together in confusion. "The rest of your family?"

"Yes, I have two uncles left alive, and they'll be joining us."

Damon doesn't elaborate, but he looks less than happy. And although I don't want to pry, I am dying to know more about his family. Partly out of curiosity, and partly out of fear. For some reason, I feel like knowing more about him may make this less scary.

At least if I know what I'm walking into I can prepare myself.

Forcing another bite of food into my mouth, I decide to ask him some questions.

"What happened to your parents?"

Damon's mood darkens, and I regret asking him. Maybe bringing up this conversation right after his asshole brother contacted him isn't such a good idea.

"I'm sorry. I shouldn't have asked. You don't have to tell me anything if you don't want to." I swallow the food in my mouth even though I feel like vomiting.

"My father wasn't what you would call *a father*. Every choice he made was for himself and his businesses. He was selfish, and he scared my brother and I in the worst ways. He did things to us no man should ever do to a child—let alone his own sons. We needed someone to protect us, but my mother turned a blind eye, as if she didn't see the fucking things he was doing.

"My mother died when we were ten, and that's when things took a dark turn." The most sinful smile I've ever seen appears on his lips, and it makes me shiver with actual fear.

"Thankfully, the fucker is dead now. A bullet to the heart will do that, though. In the end, he got what he deserved. The scars he left on my brother and I might not be visible to the naked eye, but that's because they're more than skin deep."

When I get the courage to look at him again, I see a sadness in his eyes, and I understand what he's saying. His father did this to him, trained him, taught him to be this man, and it's not something he can change—or give up. He didn't have a choice, and I'm sure he hates that.

"And your brother? Xander? What happened to him?" I hate to ask more questions, to dig deeper, but I want Damon to tell me everything. I want to know him inside and out, even if that includes learning about his sick, twisted brother.

"He took the brunt of the pain. He took the beatings, the jobs. He became father's right hand, and because of that I'll never be able to repay him. He protected me when mother wouldn't and when our father wanted to kill me."

I gasp, but Damon continues as if he didn't hear me. "But that doesn't mean I like him the way he is. I care for my brother. I care about him because he is my brother...my blood. But blood doesn't always mean family, and I hate knowing my brother is a crueler monster than our father ever was. I hate that he let our father control him, train, and groom him to be the leader of our family, and that even after our father died, Xander could have changed—he could have become better, made the family better —but he ended up becoming just like him...worse even."

I lift a hand to my throat, knowing the bruises are still there. Damon would never do that to me. He'd grab me, stop me from going somewhere, pin me down, but he'd never rip the air from my lungs. He'd never look at me with a hunger to kill.

Not the way Xander stared at me when he pinned me against the wall.

Damon clears his throat, breaking my train of thought. "He will pay for touching you, Keira. He knows you're mine, and he touched you simply because he knew it would hurt me."

"He looked at me with a desire to kill."

"And he would've killed you. I know, because he is my brother. I know what makes him tick. I know what sets him off. But he didn't because he has other plans for us. I'm not stupid. He wouldn't call a meeting like this after years of being absent from my life without having some type of plan, and he doesn't let anyone live unless they serve his purpose."

The thought terrifies me. Does that mean he'll kill Damon and I outright? I don't want to die yet, not when I've just finally started to enjoy life again. I've lost so much already—my parents, my brother. But Damon has too. He lost both his parents and technically his brother.

"Did he kill your father?" The question is on the tip of my tongue. I feel I know the answer, but I want Damon to confirm it.

"Yes. Not that the bastard didn't deserve it. It changed him, though. It made him evil." Damon sighs, and I can see the conversation is bothering him. I don't want to ruin our morning further.

Desperate to change the subject, I try to think of something else to ask. "Does it matter what I wear tonight? Is it the kind of dinner party you dress up for? Because if I'm expected to wear anything besides jeans and a T-shirt, we're going to have a problem." I force a smile, trying to lighten the mood.

Damon doesn't skip a beat. "I'll have Candy pick you up something, and you can dress at the club. I have to swing by there before dinner anyway. It'll work out perfectly."

The thought of Candy picking clothes out for me sounds scarier than going to dinner with his family. My face must reflect what I'm thinking.

"Don't worry, I'll tell her to keep the dress PG-13. Though I'd love to see you in something that shows off your body. But I don't want anyone in my family, especially my brother, to see what's mine."

My body tingles, and I have half a mind to go kiss the hell out of him, but I can see he's still facing his demons and I don't want to push him over the edge...not yet. Instead, I remain seated, feeling protected and cherished, hoping like hell we can make it through tonight and come out together on the same side.

amon

W<small>HEN WE ARRIVE</small> at Night Shift, the place is empty minus Candy and a few of my right-hand men. I'm a bundle of nerves—even though I have no reason to be. Well...sort of. I know I'll be walking into a shit-show tonight. I wonder if Keira realizes what kind of dinner to expect tonight.

Whatever my brother wants, he is going to use Keira to get it, and that annoys me. More than that, it angers me to no end, because caring for her, letting her into my life, makes me feel like I have a weakness, and that's something I've never experienced before—a weakness my brother will have no problem grabbing onto and using to prove a point.

I can feel the tension Keira carries seeping into my bones. She doesn't like the man I am when we're here, but it is what it is. I don't want to hurt her feelings.

When we make it to my office, after I do my rounds, I close the door behind us, sighing in relief. There is so much shit that needs to be done, new girls to be selected.

I need to talk to Toni and Dave and set up a meeting with all my men to discuss keeping post, since clearly it's a fucking issue being that my brother got his hands on Keira in our establishment. My head is spinning, and yet the only fucking thing I can focus on is this stupid dinner with my sadistic brother—and the fact that my hands will be forced into playing whatever game he has up his sleeve.

"Umm..." Keira clears her throat, interrupting my thoughts.

I lift my gaze to hers from where I sit behind my desk. She is in her spot on the couch—where she sat the other day...though it seems like forever ago. I've been on edge since our conversation earlier, and I'm certain she can feel it—her facial expressions confirming it.

"Yes?" I try to keep distaste from my tone. Her dark brown eyes soften me. She looks at me like I am her entire world, and I can't let her down—not today or tomorrow, never.

"We didn't..." She stumbles over her words, her teeth worrying her bottom lip, "we didn't use a condom, and I'm not on birth control."

Fuck. The thought never occurred to me. Then again, I wasn't focused on anything but making Keira feel good.

"If you're worried about catching something from me, you don't have to be. I've never fucked anyone without a condom, and I get every woman screened who works here."

"You've slept with every woman here?"

I lick my lips, not really wanting to discuss this with her. She's sensitive, far too sensitive than I have the patience for right now.

"No. I haven't slept with every single woman here. But I don't think it matters how many women I've slept with now that I'm with you." I lift a brow.

Shame fills her eyes. "Okay. I'm sorry." Her apology is full of heart, and I know she is just concerned with my feelings for her, and maybe a little worried I'll find someone else. But she has no idea what last night meant to me, or what every day being in her presence means.

"Don't be, but don't ask questions we both know you don't want answers to. I've slept with a lot of women. I have a lot of experience, but you have one thing they don't." I pause briefly, the words settling to the inside of my cheek.

I have a lot of experience, but you have one thing they don't. "My heart." I pause, panic seizing me.

"What's that?" she asks, taking a seat at the front of my desk.

I'm not ready for this moment—not even fucking close. I care for Keira, I want to protect her, but love her? I'm not sure I'm ready to admit it.

"Nothing, baby. Nothing. Forget I said anything." My voice is rough, and I hope she can't tell how raw I'm feeling. Because if she notices, if she pries, I'll have no choice but to say something that may hurt her.

Her face falls at my response, as if she was expecting me to say something else. "Okay...and what about a baby? Unprotected sex leads to babies, and I don't know what your thoughts on children are."

My thoughts on children? They're nonexistent.

The thought of having a baby couldn't be farther from my mind. Just imagining it seems odd. I don't think I can. However, for some reason, I like the idea of Keira's belly growing round and her breasts getting heavy with milk. Beyond that, I just don't know. A child...in my world...

It'd only be another person to protect—another person to hide from my enemies.

I'm about to give her some generic asshole response—like we'll worry about it later, or we'll take care of it when the time comes. But seeing her worried face, I know I need to do better. I need to be better than that...for her.

Only for her.

"We'll do whatever you want. If you want to start using birth control, I'll make it happen. If you were to get pregnant, I would be there for you every step of the way. I'm not going to leave you —if that's what you're worried about."

I can see the tension leave her body, and a relieved smile spreads across her face. This is what I want—to make her feel happy and secure—for her to know I'll go through heaven and hell for her.

A knock sounds, ending any further discussion. The smile on Keira's face falls, and I tighten my mask into place. It has to be this way.

"Come in."

The door swings open, and Gunner appears, followed by his girlfriend.

Shit, I don't need this right now.

"Hey, boss." He's making a serious effort not to look at Keira—unlike his girl who is staring holes into her face.

"Keira, are you okay?" the girl asks—the one who is clearly ignoring me—as she steps closer. And Keira gets up like she is about to hug a friend.

"Sit your ass down," I order Keira. She regards me with a pout on her lips, but does as she's told. Then I turn my attention back to this girl.

"And you, you wait outside the door." I point and glare at the girl. Now I got her attention, but she's still not following my orders. She looks back at Keira, and I catch the exact moment she sees the bruises. Her eyes widen, and her eyebrows pull together.

"Did he do that to you? Is he hurting you?" she yells, and I'm sure everyone in the club can hear.

"Lily, please...it's not like that." At the same time, Gunner steps in front of Lily, shielding her from my gaze.

"Babe, calm the fuck down," Gunner scolds her.

I grit my teeth, trying to relax myself. He better rein her in soon because my patience is running thin.

"Yeah, you might want to listen to him before I do the same to you," I snap.

Gunner visibly tenses. He knows I'm not playing games. Lily, however, doesn't get the memo—or she just doesn't care.

"No, I won't calm down. He's holding her prisoner, keeping her from coming to class, and now he is beating her? Look at her neck, Gunner!"

Feeling my patience vanish into thin air, I walk out from behind my desk and come to a stop a few feet in front of Lily.

"I can do with my property whatever the fuck I want, so if I decide I want to choke her while I fuck her, then that's what I'm going to do." I mean business now, but I refuse to look at Keira. I don't want to see the way she's looking at me right now.

Keeping my gaze trained on Lily, I stare her down, hoping to scare her enough to get her to leave, maybe even take a step back when I came around the front of the desk, but instead, she fucking lunges at me.

She's not close enough to reach me, so I don't even take a step back, but I am slightly shocked. She's got balls, I'll give her that. She doesn't get far. Gunner already has a grip on her, trying to keep her away from me. But I get the feeling that's not going to stop her.

"Jesus, Lily, calm down. Are you trying to get us killed?"

Either Lily is not hearing what he is telling her, or she doesn't give a shit. I'm going to go with the latter. Nevertheless, she's pushing buttons she has no business pushing.

She thrashes back and forth like a wild animal in Gunner's arms, and I have no doubt she will attack me again in a heart-beat if she gets loose. Out the corner of my eye, I catch Keira starting to cry on the couch. Her perfect brown eyes fill with tears, and she probably knows what I'm going to do next.

I pull my gun from the back of my pants and point it at her friend. My finger is on the trigger, ready to shoot any second.

As soon as Lily catches sight of the shiny metal of my gun, she stills. Her eyes grow wide. With my free hand, I grab cash from the drawer and throw it to Gunner.

"Get the fuck out of here before I put a bullet in both your heads. And, Gunner, from now on, you come alone—or not at all. I won't have shit like this going down in my office. My word is rule here. I won't end things so easily next time."

"Got it, boss," Gunner mumbles before dragging Lily out of the office by her arm.

The door closes behind them, and Keira is on her feet and across the room, running into my arms the next second. I pull her close to my chest, trying to absorb all her sorrow. I want to hide her from the world, protect her from everything that could hurt her—even me.

"She was just trying to be a good friend," Keira manages between sobs.

The warmth of her body seeps into mine, and I want to walk us to the couch and kiss her over and over. I want to forget about my responsibilities. I want to tell my brother to shove this dinner up his ass. I want to stay here and just be with her.

But I can't, and that's the harsh reality of the world we live in.

"I know, baby, but it's better like this. It has to be this way," I whisper close to her ear.

Even in my own club, I can't risk people hearing me talk to her like this. It's bad enough that my brother knows how important she is to me. The more people that know about her, or my feelings for her, the bigger the target on both our backs.

I hold her for a short time before releasing her. After all the things she's asked me today, I realize I never cared to ask her something in return. Probably because a part of me worries if I get too attached and something happens, it will kill me. Still... knowing little things about her can't hurt, right?

"What did Lily mean when she said I'm keeping you from going to classes?"

Keira sniffles. "I was going to college to get a degree—in what, I don't know yet; I'm still undecided—but I won't be able to return, so it doesn't matter anyway."

"Once this whole thing with my brother is settled, you can go back to classes." There will be a man protecting her on campus at all times, but we can talk about security measures later.

"I still won't be able to go." She's not looking for pity...this, I know. She's simply stating the truth.

"And why is that?"

"Because Leo paid for all of my schooling, and now that he's..." she trails off, as if she doesn't want to say the word. "I won't be able to pay for tuition, and even with a job, it's not going to be manageable. I have to eat and find a place to live too."

Shit, it never occurred to me Leo was supporting her. Paying for her schooling, her housing. It's no wonder he got caught up in some bad shit with my brother. He was trying to take care of his little sister.

He was trying to protect her—and he paid for it with blood.

"Keira, if you want to go to school, then you can. I'll pay for your tuition in full. You don't have to worry about money or paying me back. And you don't have to worry about a place to live either." Keira looks at me in disbelief.

"You can stay at my house. I've got food, heat, running water—everything you'll ever need."

"You don't mean that, Damon." She sniffles.

"Yes. Yes, I do, baby. I'll give you whatever you need to make it out of this shithole. You say the word, and I'll do it."

The words have never been more convincing. I'll do anything for Keira. Paying for her college tuition is nothing. Allowing her to live with me...nothing.

There is no cost for her happiness—not in my mind.

"I'll get everything arranged when we return from my brother's."

Oh fuck. Dinner. My brother's. I pull my phone from my pocket and check the time. We've got two hours before we need to be at the mansion.

"I'm going to call Candy. She's got your dress, and she's going to help you do your hair and makeup." I feel myself slipping back into the old me, the person I have to be. Keira must feel it too because she slowly retreats to the couch.

"Okay," she mumbles, placing her hands in her lap.

I feel the organ inside my chest beat. It's pounding, pumping blood through my body, but I can't let it control my decisions.

I need to use my head to protect Keira...

...not my heart.

eira

I STARE at myself in the mirror. Damon has me changing in the stripper's dressing room. I feel cheap, but I don't object. He has business to attend to, and he all but pushed me into Candy's arms as soon as she entered his office.

Coldness washed over him earlier, hiding all his emotions now. He's changing, reverting to his old self—slowly, so slowly. Maybe he doesn't think I see it. I don't know. I thought after last night we had made some headway...that things had changed, but...

"What are you thinking about inside that head of yours?" Candy asks while I start to get undressed. She already has my hair up in big rollers, making me look ridiculous. I hope she doesn't plan to keep these in my hair as part of the hairstyle tonight.

"First of all, I'm glad you picked this dress for me. I was worried you would choose something...um, more—"

"—like this?" She holds up one of the stripper's outfits from the nearby rack. The damn thing is made with less fabric than some of my underwear—and that's being nice.

"Yes," I giggle. "No offense, but I've never seen you in anything besides super revealing clothing, so I just didn't know what you would choose."

"Hon, I work in a strip club. Revealing clothing is our uniform. That doesn't mean I don't know how to dress for a dinner party." She winks at me, and for the first time, I wonder why she's working here. Does she like it? How does she know Damon? I think about asking, but then decide against it.

Her business is none of mine, and with the shit storm called my life, the last thing I need to be doing is questioning someone else's choices.

"Yeah, you're right. I'm sorry." I feel ashamed for judging her—when clearly my own life is in shambles.

"No, don't be, honey. It's okay to be curious and question things, but I only dress this way for the tips. The more revealing the clothing, the better the tips. Now, enough about me, why don't you let me put this beauty on you."

She holds the dark green ombre dress in front of me so I can step into it easily. She zips it up like she's been doing this her whole life, and I run my fingers against the material. It's soft and clings to my curves. It doesn't show any cleavage, but it highlights the shape of my breasts, and the collar falls over my shoulders. It fits like a glove—even though I never told Damon my size.

Taking a step forward, I look in the mirror, realizing how far the slit on the side hikes up, revealing a lot more leg than I'm used to. It's sexy, but not overly—plus, it suits the design and adds to its beauty.

My thoughts turn to Damon. I think he will appreciate this dress. After all the things he said to me in his office, I want to be any and everything for him.

"You look beautiful, Keira." Candy smiles at my reflection in the mirror. "Now, sit down over there so I can do your hair and makeup."

I tense. Makeup and hair. Oh god, it's a dinner, not a party, right?

"Don't worry, I'm not going to go crazy. No stage makeup for you, just something simple and natural. A little mascara, eyeliner, and eyeshadow. That should do the job," Candy reassures me, and I really hope she knows how much this means to me.

"Thank you. Seriously, thank you for being so nice to me." I take a seat in one of the makeup chairs, and Candy starts working on my face. I close my eyes as she starts to apply powder with a large brush, then the eyeliner, mascara, and lipstick.

"There you go. Just some blush so you don't look so pale, and your makeup is all done."

I swivel in my chair so I can look at myself in the vanity mirror. My mouth pops open, and the words I want to say are there, but they just won't come. I almost can't believe my eyes. She only used a few items, but I look so much different. Like an entirely new person.

"I'm glad you like it." Candy chuckles. "Now, let's get these curlers out of your hair and you'll be all done, Cinderella."

Just as she removes the last roller, the door to the dressing room opens. A string of high-pitched giggles fill the room. My stomach knots. Not only do I have to face the possibility of death tonight, now I have to face Damon's strippers.

I avert my eyes to the floor, and let Candy finish my hair.

"Oh my, look who it is, girls? Are you finally starting to work the stage, or are you going straight to the backroom for blowjob duty?" Hayley asks me with her nose in the air. She has bitch written all over her face, and suddenly, I realize why I left high school.

The girls flanking her must be part of her bitch-squad because they look down at me the same way.

"Just shut up and get ready for work," Candy snaps, but it's apparent Hayley doesn't care what Candy says. She blows past her and steps directly in front of me.

"You know you're just some temporary toy to Damon, right? He is going to throw you in the trash as soon as he gets bored playing with you."

Each word stabs me like a knife straight to the heart.

"He's had a lot of girls, but he always comes back to me." Her pink-painted lips twitch into an evil smile. "He's been doing it for over a year. I've been his one and only, and to this day, I'm the only one who knows how he likes it." She keeps talking, and each statement twists the knife deeper and deeper.

"You will never satisfy him like I do—hell, like any other woman." Her eyes move over my body. "You're garbage compared to us." She all but spits, and she may as well have slapped me across the face. I'm sure it would've hurt a lot less.

"Hayley!" Candy shouts, but once again, she's ignored. All eyes are on me and Hayley.

I can feel pressure building behind my eyes. Stupid tears are about to fall and mess up my makeup. I can't believe I'm letting this bitch have so much power over me, but I can't help it. Not when she's highlighted every insecurity I have and rubbed it in my face. Thoughts of Damon enter my mind he said so himself —he held back with me. He wants to fuck me hard, and I don't know if I can give him what he desires.

What if I can't and he comes back to Hayley for sex?

The thought sickens me beyond belief.

Bile rises in my throat. This is the last thing I need right now— not when I have to spend an entire evening with people who want to kill me.

"Oh, I'm sorry did I upset you, sweetie?"

When I look up at her, I want to slap that stupid grin off her face. She's close enough now that I could if I really wanted to.

"Maybe I should just teach you how to suck him off or fuck him better so you can last a little bit longer...since clearly it upsets you to know he's going to come crawling back to me." She snickers like it's the funniest thing ever—and it hurts...it hurts so bad.

I can't compose myself a second longer. The tears slip from my eyes. I know it's weak and stupid to cry over something someone says to you, but I just...I can't.

A large body walks up behind her, and I nearly flinch. The look in Damon's eyes is sinister. It promises death and destruction.

"You're fired," Damon snarls.

Hayley's eyes go wide before she turns to face Damon. As soon as she sees his face, she takes three steps backward, nearly running into me.

"Y-You don't...mean that," she stutters.

"Take your shit and get the fuck out of here!" He looks around at the other strippers. "And you all better get the fuck ready for work or else you can leave too."

Hayley clutches her purse to her chest and starts crying, but even she's not stupid enough to stand around and question him. She scurries away, pushing past Damon and through the exit door.

At the softening of his whiskey-colored eyes, I calm down, making the tears stop.

Never in my life did I think I would be happy about someone getting fired—let alone watching it happen right before my eyes. I hide my excitement of her release. I don't hate many people, but after the things she said to me, I'm confident I hate her.

I want to jump into Damon's arms and kiss him, but I know better—he wouldn't allow that, not in front of other people... especially the people who work for him. So, I just clench my fists in my lap and wait for him to say something to me.

"Come on. We've got to go," he orders, an edge to his voice. He doesn't even give me a chance to respond. He turns around and heads out the door without looking at me. My legs move on his command.

I make sure my dress is in all the right places, covering everything it should be. I catch Candy smiling at me out the corner of my eye as I follow Damon out of the dressing room. I want to thank Candy for all she's done, but I know I don't want to speak out of line. I return the smile, hoping when and if I come back, I'll get a chance.

I can barely keep up with Damon's fast pace as he makes his way through the club. It doesn't help my case of keeping up when he's almost a foot taller than me and I'm wearing heels.

I see some of the men looking at me, their eyes lingering far longer than a moment, and I drop my gaze. I want to hold up a sign that reads *Don't look at me if you value your job or life* to warn them to stop before Damon sees.

When we reach the back door, he finally stops, but by then, I'm out of breath. I suck in copious amounts of air, trying to figure out how the hell he isn't struggling. When he turns around and looks past me, checking if we are alone, I don't understand why —and then I feel his lips on mine.

His kiss is consuming and steals the remaining oxygen from my lungs. I moan into his mouth at the touch of his hands roaming my body, skimming over the thin material of my dress.

It feels like nothing separates his fingers from my skin.

When he breaks the kiss, I'm even more out of breath than before.

"You look so fucking beautiful. If we didn't have to see my asshole brother right this second, I would lock us in my office and fuck you until Sunday."

I don't really know how to respond. All I know is I'm turned on and want him to fuck me. I want him to fuck me like he wants to —not like I'm a fragile doll he's afraid he might break.

I don't care where or how; I just want him to fuck me.

"I want you." I paw at his chest, realizing he changed his clothes as well. He's looks mouthwatering in his black-on-black suit. I can tell it's hand tailored, and it fits him perfectly, making him seem bigger, meaner.

"You know I want you too. Fuck, I want you so much, my balls ache." He takes my hand from his chest and places it against his thick cock, barely restrained by his dress slacks. "But we can't. Not right now. We're already running late, and if there is one thing you will learn about my brother, it's that being late isn't tolerated."

I pout, looking up at him, wanting to kiss him, but knowing he's right.

"Okay...maybe later?" I lick my lips, anticipating his answer.

"Definitely later. Right now, we really need to go."

Damon helps me step into the Cadillac, and I buckle up. I'm nervous, and I think it's more from the unknown than anything else. The low hum of the engine fills the cab as Damon speeds down the road, heading out of town.

Most of the ride is in silence. Damon's tense, and his grip on the steering wheel has his knuckles white.

The ride is longer than I expected, and the more we drive, the less houses I see. I'm slightly terrified we'll be out in the middle of nowhere with no escape plan—or maybe that's the purpose of this entire thing.

"Where is it we're going? I haven't seen a house for, like, five miles." My eyes scan the scenery. There really isn't anything out here, nothing but road and trees.

"I can't disclose the exact location, but it's as far away. Secluded deep in the woods. My father built this place, and Xander moved back when he took over the business. I haven't been here in a few years, so I'm not sure how much it's changed."

Eventually, the car slows, and I see a huge metal gate in the distance. As we grow closer, and Damon slows down even more, the nervous knot in my belly starts to unravel. I feel like I might puke and faint at the same time.

Damon doesn't pay any attention to me as he pulls into the driveway and up to a little panel box. He types in a code, and the gate opens. The path is dark—so dark, I can barely see anything.

We drive through the gate, and I hear it close, making a loud creaking sound as it does. The noise adds to my nervousness. I feel like we're driving into a prison compound and I'm not sure when my release date will be.

Damon continues down the long driveway as if he's driving into his own personal hell. I wonder what he's thinking. What he's feeling. But I don't have the courage to ask. After a few minutes, I spot lights in the distance.

The place is huge, and I do mean huge.

"You lived here?" I gasp, realizing Damon wasn't lying when he called the place a mansion.

"Yes. And it was some of the worst years of my life."

I swallow around a knot of fear lodged in my throat. Damon pulls the SUV around a huge loop before putting it in park. I shiver, looking up the steps leading to the entrance.

This place is more than intimidating.

"I'm going to warn you now, Keira." Damon's voice is cold and almost lifeless. It scares me. "I don't know what's going to happen here. I don't know if my brother is going to try to take you away from me, or if he's going to try to kill both of us. But I want you to know I will do my damndest to protect you. I will bargain. I will steal. I will use whatever power I still have in this family to make sure we both walk out unscathed."

I force myself to breathe, knowing he means every single word.

"But I must ask one thing of you."

I nod my head without thinking twice. "Whatever you want."

Damon smiles, and it makes me feel warm inside. "Listen to me. If I tell you to do something, just do it. Trust me and my word enough to know whatever I am asking you to do is for a reason. My brother sees women as garbage—as a hole and nothing more—so if I come off as harsh or mean, that's why."

I nod again.

Got it. Speak only when spoken too.

That shouldn't really be a problem—not with how scared of his brother I am.

The bruises on my throat confirm how dangerous he is...and how stupid Damon and I are for walking right into the lion's den.

16

amon

I PUSH DOWN and swallow every single fucking emotion inside me. I cannot show weakness in front of my brother—or any other member of my family. I blink slowly, exhaling, feeling the invisible mask slip across my features.

As I open my car door, I spot my brother at the top of the steps. He's dressed similar to me, and I realize some things never change. It may have been years since we've last seen each other, but he is the same person he was when I left—and vice versa.

I walk over to the passenger side and open Keira's door. She eyes me with a hesitant glare before stepping out. Everything about Keira screams innocent—from the softness of her eyes, to the way she sees people as if they could do no wrong. She knows I'm a bad man, yet she thinks I can save her. Taking her hand into mine, I squeeze her fingers and close the door. I can feel my brother's eyes on us, and I know I need to prove a point.

Without warning, probably catching Keira completely off guard, I sink my fingers into her curls, wrenching her head back. Then I press my lips to hers. Her body shakes, and a cry of pain escapes her, filling my mouth.

I kiss her hard, bruising her lips, making certain my brother sees the ownership I have over her. When I release Keira, she wobbles, and the need to pull her close overwhelms me—but I'm not dumb enough to make such a grave mistake.

We ascend the steps together, and when we reach the top, I stand man to man with my brother.

He has a satisfied grin on his face. His eyes are dark, the color of coffee mixed with a dash of darkness like mine—hell, looking at him is like staring at my reflection in the mirror. He's only older by a few years, and his age doesn't show. He looks the same... right down to the monster flickering deep in his eyes.

I watch those monstrous eyes move from me to Keira.

"I like the way you dressed up your doll today. She's beautiful."

"She is—and she's mine," I sneer. "By the way, I enjoy placing bruises of my own on my property, so the next time you decide to touch something that isn't yours, you'll return it the way you found it."

Xander's eyes ghost over Keira's throat. "I'm sorry, little brother. I didn't mean your pet any harm. She is a fragile little thing. Her skin bruises with barely any force I see." He snickers. "However, we shall predict her future this evening and see who she truly belongs to. Until then, you can keep her at your side."

The smile on his face makes my stomach turn. Life and death are nothing but a game to him. He doesn't care who lives or dies. He only cares about making an example of someone.

Xander strolls into the house through the huge, wrought iron door. Like everything else here, this door holds nothing but bad memories. I should be thankful it holds the memories inside the house and not outside them. God forbid I let them control every single aspect of my life.

As I walk up the steps, my heart sinks. A memory slams into me so hard, it steals the breath from my lungs.

I can't believe she's dead. I stare down at my hands. She's gone. That's what Father said, but I don't believe him. She was fine this morning— happy, smiling, and now, I'll never see her again. The thought hurts. My father told me not to cry for her, and I'm doing my very best, but my eyes are burning with unshed tears.

They are going to spill over soon, proving again how weak I am to my father.

I clench my tiny hands into fists

I better go outside so Father won't see me. I run down the stairs. I think he's in the study. I can't pass him by accident.

My hand is on the brass door knob when I hear heavy footsteps behind me.

No, no, no! Treacherous tears run down my face, staining my cheeks. I try to wipe them away, but it's already too late.

"Where do you think you are going?" my father's voice booms, igniting fear deep in my belly. I hate my father...I know this to be true.

"Just outside," I say, trying to keep my voice even. Maybe if I make myself seem less conspicuous, he will ignore me.

I pull the door open and sprint outside...or try to. My father's hand is already on my neck, jerking me backward before I can take a second step.

He twists my body around so he can look down at me. His grip is harsh, and I try to stop from shaking.

"Are you fucking crying?" His eyes are daggers glaring down at me, and his fingers dig into my arms with bruising force. "And now you are trying to run from me with the proof of your indiscretion staining your cheeks?"

I don't get a chance to answer—not like there's anything I could say to make this better. I've learned to take the beatings and lick your wounds when done. The less fear you show, the less he beats you. That's what Xander tells me.

My father's fist hits my jaw, causing my head to snap to the side. I would have fallen to the floor if he didn't have an iron grip on my arm. Three or four hits follow...I lose count. If he let me go right now, I'd stay down on the floor. I'd give in, letting him win.

I'm halfway passed out, the pain overtaking me, when he shakes me awake.

"Don't you fucking pass out, you little shit. I'm not done teaching you a lesson. You take your fucking beating and learn something from it. Clearly, I need to teach you in other ways." His heated breath fans my face, smelling of whiskey. Has he been drinking? He beats us so much when he drinks.

He yanks me to the side and places my hand between the door frame and the heavy iron door. "You want a real reason to cry, then I'm going to give you one." I shake my head and try to pull my hand away, but he is so much stronger than I am.

He always is.

He swings the door open, and I squeeze my eyes shut, waiting for it to crush my hand. Then I hear heavy footfalls and open my eyes.

"No!" Xander cries, and my father releases my hand. I watch with wide eyes as Xander tries to tackle him. Xander is only fourteen, but he's big for his age, and my father can't push him around like he used to. But Xander isn't big enough to overtake father yet, so instead of proving a point to Father, he ends up below him, our father's huge body crushing his.

"Xander," I yell, wanting to save him the way he saved me.

I see him mouth the word "run," and as badly as I want to stay and help, I know when my brother tells me to do something I should do it.

"You're no better than him, Xander. Two fucking weak, pitiful excuses for men." My father's voice carries, following me as I climb the stairs to my room, locking the door. Tears slip down my cheeks.

I wish I was stronger. I wish I could protect us like Momma did.

But Momma's gone. It's just Xander and I.

Xander's voice drags me back to reality, pulling me from the horrendous nightmare.

"Our uncles will be pleased to know you actually showed up tonight."

I roll my eyes. "Oh, I'm sure they will be."

Out the corner of my eye, I watch Keira's face absorb all she's seeing. The paintings, the marble floor, the high ceilings, the chandelier, the glitz and glam—the part of my life she's never seen.

I keep a tight grip on her arm and pull her closer to my body. She nearly trips over her own feet, a gasp escaping her lips, but rights herself before doing so. Her heels clack against the flooring, echoing throughout the space. We walk through the foyer and straight into the open kitchen that leads to the garden.

The place is lit up, just as it was when we were kids.

I hear voices, two of which I know, and a few others I don't.

When we enter the room, the voices dwindle to nothing more than breath. All eyes move to Keira and watch as a soft blush creeps up her cheeks. She has no idea how beautiful she looks tonight. And she has no clue how much these evil fucking men are going to want her by the time the night is over.

"Damon." Uncle Dom, the man I'm partially named after, breaks the silence first. As he pushes from his chair to stand, the wood scrapes against the floor, causing Keira to jump. I ignore her tells and focus on the task at hand.

Dom's face is worn, a permanent expression of tired. When he smiles, it seems unnatural.

"Uncle Dom." I force a smile, letting him hug me.

He pulls back and directs his attention to Keira. His eyes reflect hunger for something other than food as he drinks her in. The gun digging into my back reminds me I could easily shoot each and every one of these fucks in the head...just for looking at her.

But I don't...I won't...at least not yet.

"And you must be Keira."

She nods, nibbling on her bottom lip. She averts her eyes to the floor as if she's submissive.

"All this trouble over such a small little thing." Dom shakes his head, as if he doesn't understand.

Well, he would, if he had a fucking heart.

"Yes, Uncle. All this trouble over Damon refusing to let go of something he doesn't actually own."

I clench my jaw. Dom must sense my hostility because a burst of laughter erupts from his throat as he slaps a hand on my back.

"Now, now, boys. You can always share her. Hell, I remember a time when you shared everything. I'm sure she could survive at least one session with the two of you before you'd have to kill her." I feel sick to my stomach, and I can practically see the horror appearing on Keira's face. Now, she's going to freak the fuck out and worry about me sharing her with my brother.

She visibly shies away. Seeing her like this is worse than getting punched in the face. I look at her, hoping she remembers everything I've told her, willing her to trust the promises I made this morning instead of believing the words I speak now.

I direct my attention to Xander. "Times of sharing my toys with you are over. You've broken them one too many times."

Memories of the last woman we shared come to mind.

"Please, no. Please, stop..." she screamed, her eyes pleading with Xander, begging for him to stop.

All I did was stand there, swirling the whiskey in my glass, having already gotten my fill of her. I can still remember the sound of her shriek as he fucked her face and placed the barrel of his gun beside her head, warning if she pulled away, she was as good as dead.

What she didn't know was that no matter what, she was dead.

Humans are disposable in my brother's eyes. The way he's watching Keira tonight reminds me of the way he watched that woman—predatory, with a purpose.

The woman's blood will forever coat my hands and my black soul. There's no way in hell I'll make that same mistake twice.

No. Keira's blood would never coat my hands.

"I can always get you a new toy if I break this one by accident," he boasts, smiling at Keira. "Though, it would be a shame to break something so fragile. She really is far too pretty to break so soon."

I watch her shudder, and I want nothing more than to wipe that smile off Xander's face with my fist.

"All right then, let's sit down for dinner and we can discuss the technicalities. There is no need to fight over pussy, no matter how good it is. There are plenty more women for the two of you to select from." Uncle Dom chuckles, like he's enjoying our little bickering match. He motions for us to follow, and we all walk into the dining room.

I have half a mind to tell Dom Keira's pussy feels like no other, but that isn't any of his damn business—none of it is anyone's business.

My other uncle, Vincent, is already seated at the table, a drink in his hand and an annoyed expression on his face. "Look who made it. I didn't think you would actually show. What's it been? Three years?"

Unlike Xander and Dom, he pays no attention to Keira. In fact, he ignores her, acting like she isn't even there—and that's perfectly fine with me.

"Hello, Uncle Vincent." My greeting sounds like a chore. This entire fucking event is a headache.

I make Keira sit on my right while Xander takes the seat beside me. My Uncle Dom sits across from us and beside Vincent. The table is set, looking like we're about to have a Thanksgiving feast. When Xander sets up dinner, it's a fucking party—an extravagant event and nothing less. I watch as some of Xander's men meander around the room, standing guard. The thought of my brother needing a guard makes me laugh.

The bastard could kill all these fucking people with his bare hands. He doesn't need a bodyguard, but the fact that he feels the need to have one is amusing.

Keira fidgets in her seat. I want to tell her to hide her fear from these men, that they will do nothing more than eat it up—but I don't. Warning her of anything that is to come is a slippery slope and will only be seen as a weakness.

"Bridget!" Xander yells, and a staff member scurries into the room. "Get my brother and the girl whatever they would like to drink."

Bridget's fearful gaze moves to Keira and I.

"She'll have a water, and I'll take a whiskey." I save my pleasantries for another time. She's not expecting a please and thank you, I guarantee it.

Bridget runs back to the kitchen, bringing the attention back to us.

"Oh, come on, brother. Can't the girl have some wine?"

"Nope. I want her coherent when I fuck her later." I don't miss a beat, and Xander chuckles.

Our drinks appear moments later, and I keep my gaze anywhere but on Keira. Tonight is going to be hard for her. I may have to do some things I'm not proud of, but I'm certain she'll leave here in one piece.

I take the glass of whiskey and down half. I don't even feel the burn as the brown liquid slides down my throat with ease. Fuck, I'm going to need a lot more of it if I plan to get through the rest of the night still sane.

The salads arrive, and we start eating. Tension hangs thick in the air like a fog. I keep peeking at Keira, but avoid eye contact. Her hands are shaking so much, I worry she might drop the salad fork. Before I reach out to steady her with a calming hand, my brother clears his throat.

"So, let's start talking business," Xander announces, setting his empty whiskey glass on the table. My uncles nod in agreement, dabbing at their mouths with their napkins.

"What business is there to discuss?" My gaze stays trained on the remaining amber in my glass. I try to sound aloof.

"Keira is rightfully mine. Her brother worked for me, then betrayed me. He stole a lot of money from me. Just before I slit his throat, he said he couldn't pay me back, but that I could have everything he owned, and clearly, that includes her." He points the salad fork at Keira, and I have to bite my tongue before I tell him to fuck off. Sparring with my brother isn't going to make this conversation smoother.

"I have to say, killing him was fun, though. I tortured him for a while to make sure he was telling me the truth—though, I suppose anyone will say what you want them to when they're staring down death." Xander keeps staring at Kiera.

I know what he's trying to do, and I hope Keira isn't falling for it. Playing into my brother's hands does nothing but feed the monster.

"He cried when I cut some flesh out of his leg. He begged me to stop over and over and over. Those are the most fun, you know —when they beg for the pain to stop. Personally, though, I loved it when he promised me *your* virginity. That was the best part— like he expected your frail, virgin body to pay for his debts."

I'm about to interject when I catch Keira's movement out the corner of my eye. She grabs the knife and lunges at Xander, her beautiful face wearing a mask of fury. Xander remains seated. His sadistic smile tells me he knows he's proved his point.

I only have a split second to decide what to do, knowing neither one of my choices is going to be pleasant. I grab her wrist first, slamming her hand on the table, making her drop the knife. She whimpers, her eyes attempting to meet mine.

I don't know why she's crying. She knows what's coming.

She should've listened to me. Fucking Christ.

My uncles are laughing like they're watching some comedian on a stage, but I know none of this is a laughing matter. Keira played right into my brother's hand, and now I'm left with no choice in the matter.

Now I have to show them I have her under control. I have to hurt her.

I grab the knife she dropped and force her hand flat onto the table. She struggles in my grip, but there's no fighting my hold. I tighten my hand over her wrist, watching as pain contorts her features. "You really shouldn't have done that."

I hoist the knife in the air and bring it down to stab her hand. I use such force, the tip of the knife embeds into the wood of the table between the knuckles of her index and middle finger.

"Next time, you'll lose a finger," I warn, releasing her wrist as I push her to the floor behind me. I don't dare look at her face. If I see her tears or even fear, my mask will crumble to the ground, giving us both away.

I take my seat, keeping my back to her. "You are done eating with us. Go upstairs to one of the bedrooms and wait for me, naked and on your knees."

I clench my jaw, and when I hear her soft footsteps leave the room, I damn near exhale in relief. She's gone. She's safe. For now. My brother has the biggest fucking grin on his face, and I decide right now I'm going to kill him someday.

"Well, that was fun," he snickers. "She's a bit of a feisty one, brother. I'm glad you've trained her well." He pauses, taking a sip of his drink. "It will make her transition into my care that much easier—since she technically belongs to me."

My uncles nod in agreement, and I clench my fists under the table. "She is mine. You won't touch her. I don't give a fuck what you had going on with her brother. She is under my protection now."

Dom shakes his head. "Damon, you know it doesn't work like this. The only way you can keep a woman under your protection is to make her family."

Why the fuck didn't I think of that?

"Fine, then I'll marry her." I don't think of the repercussions. I simply think marrying her will help her, give her the protection she needs.

Xander scoffs. I can tell he's shocked, but he doesn't let on much. Only his eyes widen a little. "You're going to marry your play thing...just to prove a point? Fuck, her pussy must be made of gold—or she can suck some good cock."

When I don't respond, he laughs. "Suit yourself...I guess, but that doesn't bring my money back. It doesn't right a wrong, brother."

I roll my eyes. "I'll pay you whatever Leo owed you, but I'm sure this isn't about the money."

I know my brother far better than anyone in the room. Money isn't what he's after. He has a reason for calling me here. He just used Keira to ensure I would follow through.

"Yes, you're correct. I don't really want the money, but there is something else I want—besides your pet."

I wait for the blow to come...

"You could start working for me again."

My blood runs cold. *No fucking way.*

Before I can utter a single word, Uncle Dom cheers, lifting his glass in the air. "Well, perfect. I'm glad we were able to come to an agreement so quickly. You get to keep your pet, and the two of you are working together again. All's right in our world, and the Rossi empire will prosper another year."

Xander smirks like the fucking monster he is before excusing himself and getting up from his seat. I know there is no point in fighting him. There's no point in any of this, actually. I basically gave myself back over to my brother—all to protect the fragile woman who owns a sliver of my heart. I did this for her. I did this for...

Love?

Another glass of whiskey is set beside me as the main course is brought to the table. I decide now that Keira is safe, I may as well drink myself into a drunken stupor. Since I just signed up to marry her—and fucking work for my monstrous brother again —I think I deserve a drink...or maybe twenty.

 eira

I THINK I may have had a mild heart attack. I clutch a hand to my chest, my heart beating so fast, it hurts. Even now, as I walk around the mansion by myself, it doesn't seem to want to slow.

I tell myself to breathe, and I do—though the action is painstakingly slow. I want to cry. I want to run out the front door and hide until it's time to leave. I'm stupid...so stupid for playing into Xander's twisted game. I should have known better than to take his bait, but he knew exactly what to say—exactly what to dangle in front of me to make me lose control.

I stroll the seemingly endless hall, feeling frazzled and stressed. Damon said to go to a bedroom upstairs—well, he should have given me a damn road map with instructions.

All the doors are closed...so how am I supposed to know where the bedrooms are? Or what rooms I can enter and what rooms I cannot.

It feels like a trap—like one wrong move and something's going to jump out and get me. I already had a taste of fear downstairs when Damon nearly took my finger off. What's the worst he could do now? Cut one off?

I open the first door to my right and pop my head in. It's dark, but the light from the hallway allows me to see this is a sitting room of sorts. I close this door and try the next. My stomach clenches. What if Damon finishes his meal and I haven't found a bedroom? Worse yet, what if his brother gets to me before he does?

With shaky hands, I twist the knob on the next door. I sigh, my eyes taking in the huge walk-in shower and clawfoot tub. Clearly, this is a bathroom, and one that's bigger than the bedroom in my apartment.

Who has a bathroom this big?

I shake my head, my feet starting to ache from walking in these heels. Leaning against the wall in the hallway, I slip them off my feet. The floor is cold against my feet, but it's a welcome feeling to my burning hot skin.

I tiptoe down the hall, stopping at another door. What I find behind it is so unbelievable, I think I might have landed in an alternate universe.

This room is unlike any other I've seen. The walls are painted pale blue. The furniture is white, and the room is lit with a nightlight that casts stars across the ceiling.

Is this a nursery?

I hold a hand to my lips. Is this...? Is this Xander's child's bedroom? No, it can't be. Maybe it's one of his worker's children? Or someone else's? There is no way Xander has a baby. No way.

A calming melody plays from a small toy sitting on top of the dresser. My feet move forward without my brain agreeing to do so. I only make it two steps before a voice drags me back to the present.

"I don't think this is the bedroom Damon was referring to when he told you to go upstairs." Xander's voice sounds like nails on a chalkboard.

Impulsively, I turn around to face him. His expression is hidden in the shadows, and I wonder what my punishment will be for crossing such a line.

"I...I didn't know."

"You ever heard the saying 'curiosity killed the cat'?"

I nod, unable to make my tongue work. My throat is completely closing up, and my pulse beats furiously in my ears.

What's he going to do?

Will he make Damon punish me? Or will he do it himself?

I want to sob as he takes a step forward, making me flinch and take a retreating step. Instead of coming for me, though, he steps around me and walks to the side of the crib.

I watch his every step. His every movement. I'm compelled to stare at him. I'm under a trance, and I can't break gaze for a second.

My body shakes as he leans over the side of the crib and takes a baby into his arms. The movement is so mundane, so simple, so gentle—for someone who isn't him, someone who has a heart and a soul unlike him. I immediately have the urge to grab the baby from him.

To protect the innocent little human from someone as evil and vile as Xander.

Courage pulses through my veins, and I take a step toward him. My intention is to stop him from hurting this baby. However, that thought leaves me when I witness something that can't be true—even though I know it is because I am seeing it with my own two eyes.

Xander leans down slowly and ghosts his lips over the baby's forehead. He's possessive and caring, and he cradles the baby's head as if he knows what the child needs and how to nurture him. They must have slipped something into my water, because there is no way in hell this can be reality.

"Why do you look so shocked?" he whispers, his voice silky and soft. It's a strange contrast to his features—since his eyes and face always seem to scream murder and pain.

With trembling lips, I ask, "Is that...? Is that your child?" If this is his child, then what happened to the mother? Why isn't she at dinner? Is she being held hostage somewhere in this mansion? A thousand thoughts circulate my mind.

When Xander takes a step toward me, I straighten my back, forcing myself to remain standing in place. I know he can sense my fear, taste it probably, but he doesn't make it known. He just closes the distance between us, bringing the baby closer to me.

In the dim lighting of the room, I can only make out some of the baby's features, but what I do see answers my question.

Cradled in a blue blanket sleeps a dark-haired baby boy. He's sleeping so peacefully, I'm afraid breathing will wake him from his happy dreams. Lifting my gaze from the baby to Xander, I realize he's watching me.

I smile. "He's beautiful."

"He is, and he's the primary reason I brought you and Damon here. His safety is my biggest importance, and just like you would do for your brother, I will do anything and everything to make certain my son is safe."

I nod, swallowing past the knot in my throat. Xander is a dark and sadistic man, but watching him hold his son, seeing how much he cares for him, proves there is a deeper, caring side to him I didn't think existed.

He walks back to the crib, kisses his son once more, and places him back down. Then he turns on his heels and heads straight for me. His facial expression is masked, and I'm afraid of what may happen next.

When his hand touches the small of my back, edging me forward, my knees buckle.

"I'm not going to hurt you, Keira. There is no point. I got what I wanted already, and my brother got what he wanted as well."

"And what is that?" I gulp, afraid to even ask. We slip out into the hall, and I let him guide me.

"You. He wanted you."

I exhale sharply, realizing Xander has figured us out. He's realized I am his brother's weakness.

"No, he doesn't want me. He just wants to use me." I stumble over my words, trying my best to make some of them sound believable.

Xander chuckles. "You're a terrible liar. Terrible." He shakes his head, stopping in front of a door to our right.

I'm not sure how long we've been walking, but I'm terrified to see what is on the other side. When he twists the knob, I squeeze my lids shut.

Xander ushers me forward, and I assume this room is his torture chamber. My legs wobble, thinking about all the pain and suffering I'm about to experience.

"You don't have to be afraid of me anymore. Yes, I am very much the monster you assume I am, but you're my brother's property now, and I will respect that. He has something he cares for greatly, just as do I. We're even now."

I open my eyes and realize I'm not being led into a killing room. I'm standing in a huge bedroom with a four-poster king-size bed.

"What happened to his mother? Did you...? Did you kill her?" I scurry away from Xander, wanting to put as much distance between us as I can. The rest of the lights in the room flicker on with my movement, and now I can see Xander's entire body.

He slides his hands into his front pockets and gives me a somber look. He appears more like a laidback businessman, and less like an unhinged murderer.

"Yes, but not because of you what you're thinking. She betrayed me. She planned on using our son against me, and I just couldn't allow that to happen."

I blink, trying to understand what he's saying. I can't wrap my head around everything I've learned tonight—and I can't wait to tell Damon all about it.

When he removes his hands from his pockets and takes a step toward me, I put a hand out to stop him. He smiles, returning to his normal self.

"Loyalty means everything to me, Keira, and even though my relationship with my brother has been turbulent over the years...my brother is still my brother. He is blood, and I will kill anyone who hurts him, including you. Do you understand me?"

I lick my lips. "I would never hurt your brother." I try to decide whether I want to tell him how much Damon means to me— how much he makes my heart sing and my body shudder.

"I love him. I love him with my entire being. Hurting him isn't something I'm ever going to do."

Xander smiles. "I know you won't hurt him, and I know you love him. I may not be as emotional as my brother, I may not show feelings at all sometimes, but I can tell you love him...simply by showing up here with him. People who love someone do things for others they may not like to do, and you clearly do for him things you may not enjoy."

"I do. I came for him—partly because I knew he needed me here, and partly because I knew you'd kill me if I didn't."

He rolls his eyes, and the look is so unnatural, I almost laugh.

Who the hell is this man?

"Dramatic much?" he scoffs. "I need an actual reason to kill you. Simply not accepting an invitation to dinner isn't one. Though... not accepting would have sped up the process of me coming back to get you—to push Damon's hand where I wanted it."

Chess. This is all a game of chess, and I suppose Xander has everything lined up, ready to steal whatever it is he wants most. He controls the entire board now.

"I'm going to go back downstairs and enjoy the rest of the night with my family. You'll be a good girl and wait up here for my brother, right? Naked and on all fours, I think he said." He winks and turns to leave.

I blush, realizing he heard what Damon said. Then again, everyone did, I suppose. It wasn't like he was quiet when he dismissed me.

"Oh, and one more thing." His eyes pierce mine, the dark orbs promising pain and misery. "Don't tell Damon about my son. He has his weakness, and I have mine, but my son is an innocent in this war—and I want him to remain hidden for as long as possible. I'm trusting you to keep this between us, Keira."

"Yes, I promise." I can't believe we are actually agreeing on something. I don't care that Xander might be a monster. That baby is an innocent in this world, and the less people who know about his existence, the better.

"Thank you." He smiles one last time before slipping out the door.

I rush to the bed and lay on it. Xander just said *thank you*. Though that's not the most shocking revelation to take place this evening. Finding out I won't be going anywhere in a body bag any time soon takes the cake.

I sit at the edge of the bed in my dress, counting down the seconds until Damon comes back. Seconds turn to hours, and eventually, my eyes grow heavy. I slump against the silky sheets, burrowing into them.

I tell myself I'll only sleep for a short time, but as soon as my head hits the pillow, I'm out, my dreams carrying me to a faraway land.

18

amon

I'M NOT sure how much I've had to drink, but by the time I stand, I'm well aware of the effect of the alcohol. I'm not wasted, but I'm definitely tipsy. I make my way to the patio overlooking the garden.

The garden is my favorite and least favorite place rolled into one. It protected me from my father when he went on his beating sprees, but it also reminds me of my entire fucked up childhood.

"Why didn't you burn the thing down to the fucking ground?" I ask, meeting Xander, watching as he takes a puff from his cigar. The sweet aroma tingles my nostrils.

"It's far too beautiful to burn to the ground. Plus, you'd miss it as much as me. Even if it is a stark reminder of our father, it's also a reminder that we had each other."

I notice a change in his attitude. He's calmer, happier, and I don't fucking like it. He's much too happy—which only means one thing: there's something going on I don't know about.

"We did have each other. When you killed dad, you changed. You took over this fucking place, and you turned it into a darker man than our father." Venom coats my words. I want him to feel all the pain I have the last couple years. But I know he won't feel shit, not without having a heart. He has no weaknesses, no fucking vices—not like me.

"You're right, I did turn into something worse than our father. I did it because I had to. I did it for you."

That's it, I've heard enough of his nonsense today. I turn to make my way back to the house. "Whatever game you're playing, I'm not going to play with you. My life was fucking perfect before you walked back into it."

I'm so pissed off, angry he dragged me here to play his sick, twisted game. It feels like we're kids all over again, except now he's holding the fact that he protected me from our father over my head.

"I'm going to bed," I mutter, walking through the kitchen, and my brother follows.

"Oh, yes..." He inhales smoke into his lungs, then exhales a moment later. "That's right, you have something waiting for you upstairs." He smirks, and my blood runs cold. "I might have left dinner a little early to help her find her way to your room, and I made sure she remembered to kneel for her king." I don't even let him finish his fucking statement. I'm so angry, so mad—at myself, at Keira, at the fucking world we live in. I stomp up the stairs, taking two steps at a time.

All I need is to see her and touch her, but as I run down the hallway leading to my old bedroom, I'm overtaken by emotions.

She's going to be my wife.

I've sacrificed everything for her, and this is how she repays me —by letting my brother show her around his mansion. I might be unreasonable, but fuck, I can't think straight right now. I'm fueled with enough madness, once I reach the door, I almost kick it in.

The lights turn on as I walk into the bedroom. I take in a sharp breath, relief flooding my veins. Keira is lying on the bed. Her hair resembles a halo, the russet-brown circling her head. She's still wearing her dress, and her tiny hands are cupped beneath her cheek.

A small wave of calmness washes over me knowing she is safe— but only from the monsters downstairs. She's not safe from me. Never me.

Walking up to the bed, I take in her perfect little body, peace-fully sleeping in a room that holds so many horrible memories for me. I clench and unclench my fists a few times, trying to ward off some of the fury inside me.

With a gentleness I'm not aware I even possess, I slowly unzip her dress and shimmy it off her shoulders. She stirs, but doesn't wake up—not even when I pull the dress all the way off her body. My mouth waters. Underneath the beautiful dress, she is wearing black lace lingerie. It makes her creamy white skin more prominent.

My dick is on high alert. I was hard earlier, but now I'm hard enough to break fucking steel.

I thought seeing or touching her would calm the anger in my veins, but now that I'm here, I feel just as unhinged. I need to have her. I need to make sure she knows she'll belong to me until the end of days.

I rip off my expensive suit, throwing it to the floor, then pull her panties down. And just when I start to climb on top of her, spreading her thighs with my knee, she wakes up.

"Damon?" Her voice is thick with sleep, but when the tip of my rock-hard cock nudges her entrance, she is suddenly wide awake.

"I'm going to fuck you, Keira. I'm going to fuck you really hard. It might hurt, but I need you right now."

All sleep vanishes from her big brown eyes, leaving nothing but panic in its wake. Part of me expects her to push me away and beg me not to do it, but she doesn't make a move to stop me— and I can't wait any longer for her to give me an answer. With one hard thrust, I bury myself inside her, all the way to the hilt.

Fuck...she feels like heaven.

She cries out in pain, but I can't stop. I'm too far gone. Consumed with need for her, my mind is clouded, and my body simply works on its own. I pull out of her tight channel, then thrust back with equal force, making her cry louder.

As she takes her bottom lip between her teeth, I peer down at her, watching her eyes squeeze shut. I catch a tear rolling down the side of her face with a kiss while I keep thrusting into her. Her salty tears coat my lips, and I drag them along her jawline before finding the sensitive spot on her neck. She smells like strawberries and me—and I want to savor and devour her all at once. I kiss her neck, moving down to her shoulder while pounding her. She cries out with each hard thrust. I worry I might be hurting her, but her cries slowly turn into a low whimper with every stroke.

Her small hands rest on my shoulders, and her fingernails dig into my flesh, scratching my skin. The sensations consume me, but I barely feel any of it. All I feel is her hot, tight pussy strangling my dick.

Mine.

She is all mine, and soon, everybody will fucking know it— when she bears my name, when her belly's ripe with my children.

The thoughts urge me forward, and I keep pounding until her cries of pain turn to cries of pleasure. I can feel her pussy gripping my cock, pulsing around me, but it's still not enough.

I can't get enough of her. I need more.

I need her deeper, harder, faster.

I pull out and get on my knees, pulling her with me. I flip her over and prop her on all fours.

Not wasting any time, I enter her again. I grip her hips and pull her toward me every time I thrust, burying myself as deep as I can. I know she's saying my name, but I can't tell if she's begging for more or begging me to stop. I hope it's not the latter, because I couldn't stop if I wanted to.

Sweat runs down my skin, coating ever part of my body. All my muscles ache, but I still can't stop. I can't stop fucking her.

After pulling her body upright until her back meets my chest, I reach my arms around and take her perfectly-shaped tits into my hands—each filling my palms just right. I take her nipples between my fingers and squeeze harshly.

Her head falls back onto my shoulder, and a loud moan escapes her lips.

Releasing one of her tits so I can touch her elsewhere, my fingers travel between us where our bodies connect until they reach her swollen, wet nub. I groan upon contact of her slippery bundle of nerves. Even if it hurts at first, I know she wants this.

She fucking wants me—even being the monster I am.

Using two fingers, I rub her clit faster and harder while maintaining the same rhythm.

"You like this?" I'm so out of breath, I barely get the words out. "You like getting fucked hard? You like me owning your pussy? Owning your entire fucking body?"

As I reach the end of my sentence, I feel her come apart. Her swollen pussy squeezes my dick impossibly tight, sending me off into my own orgasm. My balls draw together as the tingles in my spine spread through my body.

The biggest load of my life shoots from my cock into her tight little hole, filling her with my warm seed.

Keira goes completely limp in my arms. Her breathing is labored, and her head bobs to the side. I want to keep us like this forever, but I can't. I won't be able to hold myself up much longer, let alone her. I lay her down, placing her head on the pillow, then take the space beside her, pulling her into my arms as soon as I hit the mattress.

I close my eyes and listen to her breathe, wondering if she is already asleep. I'm almost certain she might be until she starts talking.

"Damon, what happened after I left dinner? Are we safe? Are you okay?" Her voice is hoarse, and I'm sure if I could see her face it would be filled to the brim with every known emotion.

"Yes, we are safe. My brother is not going to try to hurt you anymore. I made a deal with him." Her whole body goes stiff in my arms.

"A deal?" she whispers, as if it's a secret.

I know I'm being an asshole, and I'll most likely regret it tomorrow, but I just want her close right now. After all we've been through, I want her close. But more than anything, I want her to shut up and go to sleep because the voices inside my head, the demons, won't go away until I close my eyes and inhale her sweet scent.

"He wants me to work for him, and I agreed to do it." I hope the conversation ends here. But, of course, it doesn't.

"That's it? He just wants you to work for him? That's why he nearly choked the life out of me? So you would *work* for him?"

She doesn't understand the repercussions of saying no to my brother, or that her life would be on the line if I disagreed, so I'm not surprised by her lack of understanding.

"I'm working for him in exchange for your brother's debt being paid. But I had to do something else to ensure your continuous protection. I won't lose you, Keira. Not now, not ever. And...well, technically, I haven't done it yet, but I promised I would as soon as possible."

"What is it, Damon?" Her voice is shaky, and I bet she thinks I'll have to kill somebody.

"I need to get married."

Silence settles over us.

"To who?"

I can't believe she just asked me this. Does she expect me to marry someone else?

"To you, of course. We're getting married...soon. Very soon. You will officially be mine, and everybody in the world will know it."

She twists in my arms, breaking my tight grip. Her movement causes the lights to turn back on, and it's then I see the horror in her gaze.

"You're not serious, right? You didn't actually tell your family you would marry me, did you?" She seems upset. The look in her eyes tells me so. How can she be angry with me after I've given up everything for her? After all I've done to protect her? It pisses me off.

"I can't believe you're fucking mad over this. I did this for you, Keira. For us. It was either marry you or worry my family might kill you. Is that what you want? Would you rather die than marry me?"

I don't want to hear her response.

I twist away from her and shove out of bed. My head is clouded. I'm not thinking straight. I run my fingers through my hair and tug on the strands, willing my mind to work. When I turn around to face Keira, she's sitting up in bed with the comforter pulled to her chest, her eyes full of worry.

"No. That's not what I want, Damon. I don't want you tied to me forever—not when you can't tell me you love me."

I want to laugh. Actually, I want to destroy this fucking room and all its contents. But I'm tired...so fucking tired.

My gaze drops to the mattress, and I see blood. It sticks out on the white bed sheets, and I nearly vomit on the floor realizing I've truly become a monster.

I fucked her hard enough to make her bleed. If I was Keira, I'd hate me too.

I wouldn't want to be married to a monster, but she doesn't have a fucking choice—and neither do I.

Keira's eyes follow mine, and the horror in her gaze mirrors my own. She hides her facial expression as soon as she realizes the way she's looking at me, but not fast enough. I've seen it, and I'll do anything in my fucking power to make certain she doesn't have to look at me that way again—ever.

I can't do this.

I can't lose her.

I don't deserve her.

But I don't care if I deserve her.

She's mine and always will be.

I walk into the attached bathroom and turn on the water in the garden tub, making sure it's the perfect temperature before I pour in the bath salts. When I walk back to the bedroom, Keira is still sitting right where I left her. Her eyes lift to mine as I enter the room.

Her expression is inscrutable. I pull the comforter from her grip and reach for her naked body. I pluck her off the bed, cradling her to my chest. She's a little tense, and I hate that I'm the reason. Holding her in my arms, I'm reminded of how little she weighs and realize I sent her upstairs without dinner.

Fuck, this whole marriage thing isn't getting off on the right foot. Bringing her into the bathroom, I lower her into the hot water.

"Can I leave you here a few minutes? I need to get you something to eat."

"Yeah, I'll be fine. I'll be here when you get back" She seems surprised, maybe even astonished, that I'm going to get her some food in the middle of the night. She better get used to it.

If she's going to be my wife, I'm going to take care of her any way I possibly can.

Leaving Keira behind to enjoy her bath, I pull on some shorts and head downstairs. Walking through these hallways in the middle of the night awakens feelings I thought I had buried long ago.

Picking up my pace, I make my way to the kitchen and head straight for the fridge without bothering to turn on the light.

I find some leftovers—a few pre-made sandwiches and some fresh cut fruit. I pull out a small tray from the cabinet and pile it on. It's so fucking weird that nothing seems to have changed.

Every item in the house is in the same location. Just as I close the fridge and place two bottles of water on the platter, I hear it: a faint cry echoing through the house.

For a moment, I panic, thinking it's Keira, but then I realize it sounds more like a child...a baby even, and I pause. My ears strain to hear more cries, and I turn my head toward where I think it's coming from.

Then it stops.

Shaking my head, I take the platter and make my way upstairs.

I must have had a little more to drink than I thought.

A baby? In this fucking house? That's hilarious.

I push the stupid thought away, and by the time I enter the bathroom, the tub is filled all the way. Only Keira's head is above the water.

I set the tray down on the counter and pick up a sandwich. Kneeling beside the tub, I hold it in front of her mouth, urging her to eat. She eyes it curiously before taking her hands out of the water to grab it.

"No, I'll feed you. Your hands are all wet and soapy. Plus, it's the least I can do after..." my voice trails off. I know she came. I felt her pussy gripping my cock, but it doesn't make the fact that I treated her as badly as one of my fucking lays back at the strip club, or how I treated her after dinner. She means more than that to me.

"Please stop. It's okay, Damon. It's not like I didn't enjoy it too." She smiles softly and lets her hands fall below the water while she opens her perfect mouth to take a bite. Her pink tongue darts out over her bottom lip, and I want to kiss her instead of feed her right now.

"If you don't like this, I brought a variety of foods you can try."

"I see that." She smiles while chewing. "This is really good. I like it."

I feed her the whole sandwich, bite after bite, and I don't know how, but my cock starts to harden all over again. I had no fucking clue feeding someone could be so erotic.

But, fuck, it is. The way her plump lips form around the bread, grazing my fingers...it's so fucking sexy. I want to fuck her again. Now.

I tamp the need down, though, and grab the bottle of water, twisting off the cap. I hand it to her and watch her finish almost the whole bottle.

God, I am horrible. Clearly, she was hungry and thirsty. I should've taken care of her needs before taking care of mine, and for that, I am a prick—a big ass prick.

"I'm sorry, baby. I'm sorry. I was a selfish prick tonight. I should've made sure you had food and water sent up." I lean over the tub and press a soft kiss to her forehead. "It won't happen again."

Keira sighs, sounding as if she's enjoying the luxury of being pampered, and I must say, I'm enjoying it too.

I grab a washcloth from the cabinet under the sink, then kneel back down beside the tub. She rests her head on the rim and stares at me in awe as I take the cloth and start to wash her body.

She closes her eyes and lets out a low moan, sounding as if this is the best thing she's ever felt. I will have to make note of the things she enjoys so I can do them more often.

As I wash lower down her belly and between her legs, I am extra careful my movements are slow and graceful. I watch for any signs of discomfort. Her eyebrows pull together, and her delicate features tense up as I brush the washcloth over her thigh.

She is trying to hide that I hurt her, and I don't understand why —not when we both know I see it. Her teeth sink into her bottom lip, and she whines when I go over the sensitive area.

Seeing the pain in her eyes makes me want to stab myself in the heart a hundred times. She is so fragile—so fucking innocent in every way—and I took her like a fucking savage. I tore her from the inside out, making her bleed. My insides feel like they're being ripped from my body. I should've stopped. I should've taken her slower. I should've prepared her. Made her come once or twice. But I was so caught up in the need to make her mine, everything but my lust for her slipped my mind.

"It's okay," she tells me, as if reading my mind.

Her words make it worse. She is trusting me with everything— with her life, her body, her heart. And I've done nothing but fail her. It's me who's responsible for her safety now. Me who's supposed to make sure no one hurts her. Above all, it should never be me that hurts hers. I slow my movements and pull the washcloth from the water. There's a red tinge on it, and I squeeze my eyelids shut, tossing the fucking thing over my shoulder.

"It's not okay, and it won't happen again. It shouldn't have happened at all. And it will not happen again." I say it more to myself than her. She doesn't control my body, or my fucked up mind, so it's not her fault I lost my cool.

"But I want it to happen again."

I shake my head, the frustration in me mounting. "You don't mean that, Keira." I run my knuckles along her cheek, feeling how fragile her skin and bones are beneath my touch. I've killed people. I've bathed in their blood, but when I'm with Keira, I want to forget that part of myself. I want to cherish and hold her.

I stare down at her. "You don't have to pretend with me. I'll protect you no matter what, no matter how. You don't have to pretend you like being hurt because you're scared."

"I'm not scared," she admits with a shy grin. "I just...I want you to be satisfied, and I want to be the one satisfying you. I don't want you to feel like you have to go somewhere else for your needs—even more so now that I know we're getting married. I want to be able to take whatever you give me...whenever you want."

"Is this about what Hayley said? Did she tell you I didn't want you? That'd I'd leave you?" Anger doesn't even begin to describe how I am feeling.

"Listen to me, Keira." I grip her chin firmly now. "Don't fucking believe a single word she says. She's no one. A fucking whore. And not that it matters, but this has nothing to do with being satisfied. I was satisfied making love to you. I was satisfied fucking you...being inside you. Hell, I was satisfied just with the simple fact that you let me touch you."

Her eyes fill with tears. "But there's a difference between all those things and tonight. The difference has everything to do with me and the fact that I let my anger get out of control. I let it cloud my thoughts and my judgement. And I took that anger out on the one person who didn't deserve it."

I feel my own eyes begin to water, but I blink the emotions away. "I hurt you, and I'll never let myself get that out of control again. I'll find another way to manage, but it won't mean fucking you when I'm that far gone."

She gives me the sweetest smile I've ever seen, and I lean down and press my lips against hers tenderly. My heart starts beating out of my chest, and the pain of what I did pumps through my veins. I knew when she first told me she loved me I loved her too. I was just too weak...to consumed with fear to say it.

But after tonight, I won't hold back anymore. I let the words fall helplessly from my lips. "I love you, Keira. And I cannot wait for you to become my wife."

 eira

His words replay on repeat. *I love you, Keira...*

Shock isn't even a word I could use to describe or explain how I feel. I'd been saying I love you to him for a while, but I didn't think he would actually say the words to me—and never out loud.

It's like he's changed. Something inside him has cracked, and he's finally slipping his mask off and letting me in. He's been acting like he cares for me—but is it love?

I didn't think it was possible for a man like Damon to admit he was is in love. Yet, here we are, in the bathroom of this giant house where he grew up with his brother, his tiny little secret right down the hall. If Damon was ever going to tell me he loved me, I didn't suspect it would happen here.

"Come on. Your hands are turning to prunes. Let's get you dried off and into bed."

As I stand, I notice my legs are still weak, causing my knees to threaten to buckle beneath my weight. I was seriously exhausted before stepping into this hot bath, and now my muscles are relaxed, making me even hungrier for sleep.

When I step out of the tub and into the large, fluffy towel Damon is holding out, the soreness between my legs flares, reminding me of the rough way he took me earlier. I was shocked at first—and he did hurt me in the beginning—but once my body adjusted, I enjoyed the way he took me.

He was hot and possessive, and he made my body shake with need. The orgasm was mind blowing. I'm so confused by the way he made me feel, I don't think I can explain it to Damon in a way he'll understand—at least not tonight. But I do hope he does it again, because there was something so primal about the way he wanted me, needed me. Like he had to have me. Thinking about it makes my muscles clench and my body hum.

I realize we, once again, didn't use a condom, and my mind shifts to the secret down the hall.

When will Xander tell his brother about his son? How long will I have to keep this secret from Damon?

Damon's touch pulls me from my thoughts as he wraps me up in the towel, pulling me into his chest. As he starts to dry me off, I thank the good Lord for delivering a man to me who I consider to be one the best alive. My eyes comb his well-defined upper body, his shoulders and the cords of muscles in his throat. His biceps flex, and my core clenches. My gaze slips lower over his abdomen and down to his V. His muscles tighten with every move he makes, and I can't stop the urge I have to reach out and touch him. I want to feel him under my fingertips.

I trace his pecs, enjoying how smooth and warm his skin feels and how hard the muscle is beneath it. It's so small, I almost miss it, but when my fingers go back over the same patch of skin, I notice a small blemish—an abnormality on an almost perfect surface.

"What's this?" I trace the small indentation, becoming aware Damon is done drying me off and now staring down at me as I feel him up.

"It's a bullet wound," Damon says, as if it's obvious I'd know that.

"Yeah. I gathered that it was a wound. Why? Who shot you?" I have a fierce need to protect Damon—which is strange since he can kill with his bare hands. I love him, and the thought of someone shooting or hurting him bothers me a lot.

He tosses the towel over his shoulders, pads out of the bathroom, brushing past me, and I worry he may not give me an answer.

As fast as my legs allow, I follow behind him, watching as he walks to his dresser and pulls out a T-shirt and a pair of boxers.

"Here, you can sleep in these. I forgot to bring the luggage inside, and I don't want to go back out to get it." He gives me a soft smile. "Hope that's okay."

I narrow my gaze. "Who shot you, Damon?"

His eyes darken. "I don't think you're ready to hear the dirty details about my family, baby. We're a seriously fucked up crowd, and I intend to keep you as far away from it all as I can."

For as long as I've known Damon, I've been a pushover. I've allowed him to sweep things under the rug, but if I'm going to marry him and make it through a life with him, then I'm going to need to tighten my backbone. I'm going to need to say what I want to, when I want to.

"It's a little late to save me from the gory details. I know things now. Things that can't be unseen or unheard." I soften my voice. "And I know it's in the past—a past that doesn't include me—but I am part of your life now, and if you're seriously going to marry me, I'll be part of your future for a long time. I want to protect you like you protect me. I want to hear about your problems... your fears. I want to be your equal. So, dammit, just tell me."

When my eyes meet Damon's. I expect to see anger, maybe even fury, but there's humor in his gaze and smile.

"I don't know how you do it, Keira, but you make me fucking want you more and more every day. It's sickening and terrifies the fuck out of me."

His response warms my heart and makes me smile. I cross the room and get dressed in the items he set out, waiting impatiently for him to tell me. I have to roll the boxers more than a couple times to get them to stay on my waist, and when I pull on his shirt, it lands at my knees. I feel and look like I've been swallowed by cotton.

When I settle onto the mattress, Damon sits beside me and reaches for my hand—like he needs to be touching me in some way to tell me this story. I don't mind. His touch is comforting, kind, and I love that he's finally showing me his different sides. He reminds of a kaleidoscope. I see a different shape and color every time I look, and then they become clearer.

"My dad shot me. That scar is from the bullet. It was the same night Xander shot him."

Damon's gaze seems far away, and I wonder if he's thinking back to that night.

"Actually, it was the reason Xander shot him. My father tried to kill me. He wanted Xander to do it. When my brother refused, my dad shot me instead. It's a good thing he's a lousy shot. If not, I'm sure I wouldn't be here today." He grins, but it makes me feel sick. I'm sure he's smiling to lessen the blow, but it doesn't. Unfortunately, he can't protect me from all the bad in this world.

At least his father is dead...I guess.

My chest hurts thinking about what Damon must have went through. His own father tried to kill him, then their father died by the hands of his brother—right in front of him. It sounds horrendous and makes my life problems seem mediocre.

"I'm sorry." I give him a somber look and squeeze his hand tightly, as if that will take his pain away.

"I am, really. I'm sorry we had to come here. I can't imagine what being here in this house has done to your head."

Damon shrugs. "It's okay, Keira. I don't want your pity. I wanted to come here, and it was worth it. You make every hard thing worthwhile. If you didn't bring me back here, it would've been my brother with his asshole ways, so don't feel bad, baby."

Damon pulls me into his arms and drags me to the bed. We cuddle up in the heavy comforter, and I bask in the feeling of him holding me like this. It feels so good, I almost don't want to go to sleep.

The last thing I think about before sleep finally claims me is how Damon's story gives me a newfound appreciation for Xander. Discovering all I did about him tonight shows me there's more than one side to him—sides he's trying to hide from the world. The question is: will he ever find someone to pull him out of the darkness he tries to hide himself in?

 amon

THE GIRL ON THE STAGE—WHATEVER her name is—dances around the poll aimlessly. She's uncoordinated and looks like she might barf. She also can't hold my attention for longer than two seconds, so why the fuck would I hire her?

I take a calming breath through my nose and exhale out my mouth.

I look back over my shoulder at Keira sitting at the bar with my laptop in front of her. She finally re-enrolled in classes, and we agreed until I can get a man I trust to guard her, she will take only online courses.

I can't believe how attached I am to her. Normally, I couldn't care less for a woman, but Keira isn't just any fucking woman.

She is *the* woman.

My soon-to-be wife.

My world.

I turn back around in my chair and hold a fist to my head. This is the first time I've been back at the club in almost two weeks, and it's only because I had to hire some new girls.

No one here knows about our engagement—mostly because I don't share my personal life with the staff—and because it's no one's fucking business. I'm not hiding, but I'm not going to put an X on her fucking back for being hitched to me.

The door opens next to the stage, and three of my best dancers walk in. They smile brightly at me as if I'm going to cut them a bigger paycheck for doing so.

"All right. You, you, and you." I point to the top three girls who auditioned. "These are three of my best dancers. They're going to show you the night routine. If you can keep up, you're hired. I'll let them be the judge."

My eyes drift to the remaining girls. "The rest of you are welcome to audition again later in the year."

Two of the girls frown, and the other flips her hair over her shoulder like I inconvenienced her. If this place didn't make me so much fucking money, I'd burn it to the ground and start over.

I scrub a hand down my face. I want a drink. It's not late enough in the day, though.

Seconds after the rejected chicks walk out, a long-legged blonde in a pencil skirt walks in, carrying a bunch of folders.

"Hello, I'm Maria, the wedding planner," she announces, setting off a chain of giggles from the girls who know me.

The woman looks shocked as she notes the half-naked girls near us. I'm sure this doesn't happen every day in her line of work.

"Sorry, lady, you're at the wrong place if you think someone is getting married here. This is a strip club, not a church." Georgia snickers, her eyes dazzling with amusement.

I shake my head. She has no fucking clue how wrong she is.

I get up from my chair and hold out my hand. "Don't mind them. You're in the right place. We've talked a couple times on the phone. I'm Damon."

"Nice to finally meet in person, Mrs. Rossi?" She seems confused for a moment as she addresses Georgia, clearly thinking she's Keria. "I brought everything you asked for, and I just need you to choose from the selections."

"Keira," I call out, my voice gentle. I turn around and find her standing right beside me. "Why don't you take Maria to my office where you can have some more privacy? If you need anything, let me know."

"Sure, this way," Keira beams and leads her to the back.

My gaze flickers to the girls on stage. I expect to find them dancing, but instead, they are all looking at me like I lost my fucking mind.

Jesus Christ. I definitely need a drink. As I sit back down in the chair, the side entrance door opens again. Diego fist bumps Hero as he walks through the door.

I smile. "Hero, you just missed the show. We had some great girls audition today. Would've been nice to have your help selecting a few." I smirk, wiggling my eyebrows. Elyse walks closely behind him.

He shakes his head, disgust filling his features. "Next time. Maybe."

Elyse apparently doesn't think anything I've said is funny and elbows him in the ribs. He holds his side, pretending it hurts, and I almost roll my eyes. As much as I hate affection of any sort —except showing Keira love—I really do care for Hero and Elyse...which is weird to think about since I tried to kill Elyse at one point.

"Keira just took the wedding planner lady to my office. They're making final decisions today or something," I tell Elyse with a shrug. I pretend like I have no clue what's going on, but I've helped Keira select everything she wanted for our wedding, down to the damn napkin color.

Elyse smiles, but I still see the lingering sadness in her eyes. Even though me helping track Hero's father down probably saved her life, I still don't think she likes me very much, but she tolerates me, and that is good enough in my eyes. She's been through hell and back, and I cannot imagine how I would feel if something like what happened to her happened to my Kiera.

"Yay. Let me go help them then." Elyse gives Hero a kiss on his cheek before heading toward the office.

Hero sinks into a chair beside me and watches Elyse walk away. Once she's out of earshot, he speaks. "I've never really thanked you for what you did that day. I mean, without you, I might have gotten there too late." I hear the anguish in his voice. Finding her like that broke him, ripped him apart inside, almost more than killing his stepfather.

"You're welcome."

"While she was in the hospital, we found out she's pregnant."

My eyebrows lift in surprise at his confession. Holy fuck, Hero is going to be a father? The idea seems ridiculous, but the more I let it sink in, the more it makes sense. Hero and Elyse are having a baby. Keira and I are getting married. Two ideas that would have been nothing more than a joke a few month ago are now a reality.

"Congratulations, Hero." I slap his back, recalling when he told me loved her. How stupid I thought he was. Now look at me. Funny how karma comes around.

Hero smirks. "You're next."

I shake my head. "No. I want to enjoy Keira for a while on my own." I don't dive into the technicalities of the marriage. I'm sure Hero has thought up his own reasons for it, reasons that probably make me look crazy as hell being that the last time he saw me with her I was a raging dick.

"I didn't think I'd want kids. Like ever. Not after everything with my own father."

I clench my fist, understanding far fucking more than he thinks. "Love changes people," I state, looking him head on.

"Sure fucking does," he chuckles.

I guess it's never too early for a glass of whiskey—not with all the happiness surrounding us. It's almost like we're fucking normal, instead of overrun with crime and drugs.

"Candy, bring me two glasses of whiskey, please," I yell over my shoulder.

Hero's eyes go wide. "When did you start saying please?"

I grit my teeth. Fuck, he noticed.

"Recently. I'm trying to be fucking nicer to people. Not everyone deserves my dick tendencies—or at least that's what Keira says."

I can tell Hero thinks it's funny as hell, but he's just as whipped and in love with his woman as I am.

Candy appears with two glasses of whiskey. I grab one and hand the other to Hero. He eyes me for a moment, waiting until Candy is out of earshot, then he lifts his glass for a toast.

"To being pussy whipped." The shit eating grin is a permanent fixture on his face, and I can't fucking believe I'm toasting to this.

I shake my head and raise my glass to his, and we clank them together. "To being pussy whipped."

The whiskey burns my esophagus, blanketing my belly in warmth.

"Are you excited to be married?" Hero asks after downing his drink in one gulp. He wipes his mouth with the back of his hand. He's still working for me, but not as much as before—and I understand why now.

I shrug. "It's marriage. I doubt anything between me and Keira will change."

"Do you love her?'

His question hits me right in the chest. I've never confessed to anyone but Keira how much she means to me. I don't plan on hiding it from anyone, but I don't want to make it known either.

If hiding my feelings from everyone but her protects her, then that's what I'll do.

"Yes. At first, I wanted to hate her because she got under my skin and refused to listen to me." I think back to how big of a pain in the ass she was.

God, she was a thorn in my side.

"Yeah, I can relate. Our women fight tooth and nail even when we're trying to do the right thing by them."

"That's what we should've toasted."

Hero laughs. Then the ringing of my cell interrupts our conversation. My mood sours as soon as I see Xander's name flash across the screen.

"What?" I growl, trying to sound as annoyed as possible.

Of course Xander completely ignores my attitude—which pisses me off even more.

"Damon, I need you to come to the mansion. We have some important matters to discuss, and you should bring Keira as well."

It's enough that he's commanding *me*. Now he wants to tell Keira what to do as well.

My annoyance turns into anger. I hate that he has such a hold over me. I need to find a way out of this mess. But for now, it will be best to keep him happy.

"We'll be there tomorrow night."

"I would prefer you come today."

He's not asking, he's telling.

But I have something with Keira planned—something far more important than meeting my brother's needs.

"Well, I'd prefer not to come at all, but we both know how that would go over...so how about we come tomorrow?"

"Suit yourself." His tone is clipped.

My mouth pops open—a response is on the tip of my tongue—but I don't get to say shit because, like always, the bastard hangs up.

What the fuck was that?

I shake my head, slipping my phone back into my pocket. If I look confused, Hero doesn't say shit.

"All done," Keira chirps behind me. When she comes into view, I see a huge smile on her face. Her eyes are bright and full of happiness. I hide my features and smile back at her. The unease I feel from talking to my brother consumes me.

My brother's a dick, but he doesn't do shit or ask for shit unless it's truly needed.

Maria joins us. "Yes, Mr. Rossi, we are all set. This will be a beautiful wedding. I think you will be very pleased with the outcome."

Of course. After all, she's getting a big fat paycheck when this is over.

I've drowned out the dancers on the stage—as have Hero and Keira. Maria and Elyse, however, are clearly uncomfortable with the half-naked girls dancing in the background.

"Well, if no one needs anything else, I guess we'll see each other at the wedding."

Maria tries to hide her discomfort by being overly chipper. Armed with her stack of folders and books, she walks out the door like she can't get away fast enough.

Watching her leave reminds me I want to get out of here too. But boss duties will keep me here most of the day. The excitement of what's to come tonight eases some of the tension from my veins.

I've got it all now. What could possibly go wrong?

I CAN'T BELIEVE how fucking nervous I am. It's just a stupid ring. It's not like I'm asking her to marry me. So why does it feel like someone kicked me in the stomach ten times?

I wipe my sweaty palms against my dress slacks. She's already agreed to marry me—not that she has a choice in that matter. Even if she said no, I'd still make her mine. I grab the little black velvet box from my pocket.

Keira is curled up on my couch, reading a book. I had planned on giving her the ring at dinner, then at dessert, and then I pushed it back to...when we arrived at the house.

I feel sick to my stomach, thinking she may not like it. Maybe I could give it to her after she's done reading. It'd be rude to interrupt her, right?

Fuck this, I'm being ridiculous. I just need to do it.

I waltz over to her, and she looks up from her book, confusion written all over her delicate features.

"I got you something." I pull out the box, then sit down next to her. "I hope you like it." I swallow my anxiety. Her eyes go wide, and understanding settles onto her face , as a softness takes over her features when I hand her the tiny black box.

She doesn't say anything until she flips open the top and sees a two-carat diamond ring set in a white gold band.

"Damon," she gasps, her hand clutching her chest. "It's beautiful."

"You really like it? We can get something else if you don't." I rub the back of my neck. My cheeks heat. Fuck...how long has it been since I felt this way?

Keira gazes up at me, her mouth gaping open. "Are you kidding me? It's stunning. I love it! We're not returning it, and we're not getting anything else."

I take the ring from the box, grab her hand, and slide it onto her slender finger. Thanks to Candy's trickery, I obtained Keira's ring size without having to ask...thank fuck. Simply so I'd be able to see this moment as it should be seen. Her eyes sparkle as she tears up. She looks at her hand a few more moments, then throws them around my neck and crawls into my lap.

I hold her tight against my chest, burying my nose into her hair so I can breathe her in. She's soft, and I run my hands up and down her body. I want to strip her bare and hold her close while I move in and out of her with a rhythm that might kill us both.

My lips are seconds from pressing against her skin when the fucking doorbell rings.

Who the fuck has the balls to ring my doorbell?

It rings so seldom, I hardly know what it sounds like, but right this second, I want to disable the fucking thing and rip it from the front door.

"Wait here," I mumble against her hair. It's probably nothing, maybe a Girl Scout selling cookies, but I'd rather check and be safe—especially when it comes to Keira.

I'm irritated as fuck. My fists are clenched. Fucking people are always ruining shit. Once I look through the small pane of glass and see who it is, my annoyance reaches a newfound height.

Motherfucker. No.

What the fuck is she doing here?

I yank the door so hard, I worry I might break it. I open my mouth to tell her off, but I can't even get a fucking word in.

"Damon, I've been trying to reach you." Hayley's high-pitched voice makes my ears start to bleed.

"And the fact that I've ignored every one of your calls and texts didn't make it clear enough for you?" First, she fucks with Keira. Then she shows up on my doorstep and ruins my fucking night. And for what?

"Just...just give me a chance. I'll do whatever you want. I'll let you fuck me whenever you want."

Tears swim in her eyes, and I might be a cold, callous asshole, but I don't care.

"Get the fuck off my property before I have you removed."

Hayley shakes her head, hiccupping as she takes another step forward. I'm seconds away from slamming the door in her face when she rushes me. Her small frame slams into mine, hardly moving me, but it's enough for her to gain entry.

It's not her throwing herself at me that causes me to lose my fucking mind, though; it's her lips crashing into mine. Disgust and anger fill my veins, and without even thinking, I push her away, wiping my mouth with the back of my hand.

I'm not one to hit women, but I really, really want to fucking hit Hayley right now.

She steadies herself as if she's prepared for me to push her, and then I see it—the metal glint of a gun pointing in my direction. I can disarm her in a second, but it takes less than that for a bullet to release from the chamber.

She points the gun at me, and I don't even flinch.

"It's because of her, isn't it?" Hayley screams and looks past me.

I glance over my shoulder looking, following her gaze. When I find Keira standing a few feet behind me, I nearly come unglued.

My heart pounds out of my chest. Fear cripples me when I hear the click of the safety being released and see Hayley pull the trigger.

There's no way I can stop the bullet—no way—but I still lunge for it. Everything happens impossibly fast, yet I feel like I am moving in slow motion. I'm trying to shield Keira with my body, but I am too slow. I feel the bullet whizzing by my head before I hear the bang. I'm so close to the gun, I can't hear anything but a ringing in my ear. My head swings back to Keira. She looks scared and shocked, but unharmed. Relief hits me like a wave, but then washes away just as quickly.

Keira is still in danger. I turn back to Hayley. I am right in front of her—fully shielding Keira. The gun is still pointed at me, but Hayley makes no move.

Anger like I've never felt runs through me as reality settles in. She shot at Keira. She fired a gun at my soon-to-be wife. All-consuming fury floods my veins, shutting down common sense and reasoning, leaving me to act on pure instinct. My most primal instinct tells me to protect what's mine.

I close the distance between me and Hayley with two long strides. All the blood drains from her face. Her hand is shaking so fucking hard, she drops the gun.

Her eyes are so wide, they look about to come out of their sockets. I can see her mouthing, "Please," but I'm too far gone to register her pleas—or even care.

My hands move effortlessly, of their own accord, wrapping around her thin neck. I grab the base of her skull. My fingers dig into her flesh, and with one hard twist, I feel her bone crack as I snap her neck.

I peer down at her face. Her eyes go vacant in an instant, frozen in time, never to blink again. Her body goes limp in my hands. Adrenaline courses through my veins. My heart races furiously.

As soon as I realize she's dead and I have eliminated the threat, the fog of fury lifts, allowing me to think for the first time in minutes.

Shit. I just killed her in my house...with the front door wide open. *Fuck.*

My house is fairly secluded—covered by trees and bushes. But there's still a chance someone could've seen us, and even if they didn't, they certainly could've heard the gunshot.

I drag her farther inside and shut the door.

Only then do I let go of her, and the lifeless body falls onto the hardwood floor with a thump. I gaze up at Kiera. She's still standing in the same spot—her entire body has turned to stone.

"Keira, it's going to be fine." Even I'm surprised at how low and calm my voice sounds. Holding my hands up, I walk toward her slowly, like I'm trying to sneak up on a wild animal. Her eyes are fixated on Hayley's body until I step into her line of vision, blocking her view.

God, I wish she wouldn't have seen me do that. And yet I don't feel a smidge of guilt. Only guilt that my sweet Keira had to witness it.

I gently place my hands on her shoulders—the same hands that killed someone a few minutes ago. I've killed for her now. And given the chance, I'd do it again if it meant she'd remain safe.

I expect Keira to pull away and run, but she makes no moves. Her eyes move from my chest to my face. I see fear leave her gaze when our eyes meet, relief flooding her features.

In an instant, she leans into my body, her tiny arms wrapping around my middle.

A sob rips from her throat, and she cracks straight down the middle.

"Everything is going to be okay, baby. No one is going to hurt you. I need to make a phone call, and then we are going to go somewhere."

"You could've died." It sounds like her heart is breaking, and then I realize what she said. *I. Could've. Died.*

Those three little words nearly send to my knees After all she witnessed, watching me kill a woman right before her eyes, and she's worried about *me* dying. She's worried about me fucking dying. My heart soars from my fucking chest, and I reach down and pick her up, placing my hands under her ass.

I hike her up my torso, and she wraps her legs around my middle with little effort. I carry her into the kitchen and settle her onto the counter, inserting my body between her legs. Her face is still buried in my neck, each little breath she takes fanning my skin.

As badly as I want to calm her down, nothing I say is going to help until I get Hayley's body out of the house. I pull out my cell and glide my fingers across the screen, pulling up Toni's info. I hit the green call button and bring the phone to my ear.

Keira pulls away slightly, her brown eyes peering up at me.

"Boss," he answers casually.

"I've got a body I need dumped. It's at my house."

"Sure thing. I'll be over with the men in just a few."

I hit the end key and pocket my phone. I can't imagine being in Keira's shoes. These things are normal to me. I've seen more people die than be born, so death is nothing to me. Calling Toni to remove a body? Normal.

It's normal to Toni too—just another day of work. But to Keira, my fragile beauty, it's not, and I don't want her to ever look at me differently for the things I did tonight.

"Are you okay?" I lean down, inhaling her sweet scent. I'm so far gone, so fucking in love with this woman, I'd burn down the fucking world. I'd kill anyone or anything that tried to take her from me.

"Yes, I'm just..." Her lips tremble as she tries to speak. "I was afraid I might lose you back there. Afraid she was going to take you from me."

Her fear is understandable, but she doesn't have the slightest clue how badly it could've ended.

"She didn't come here to shoot me, baby. She came to shoot you." I trail my thumb over her bottom lip. "And I was going to be fucking damned if I let her succeed. You are my all—my start, my middle, and my ending. She tried to take you from me, so I ended her life. Nobody fucks with what is mine. Nobody."

Keira fists my shirt. "I was just...I was scared."

I cup her cheeks. Her skin is warm and wet with tears. "No one is ever going to take me from you. The fact that you care more for me than yourself, or that I killed someone right before your eyes..." I shake my head. "It rattled me to the core, baby. You're selfless, and your kind and caring nature makes up for everything I lack."

Keira's frown turns into a soft smile, and I lean down, pressing my lips against hers. Her head falls against the cupboard, exposing her smooth neck. I want to fuck her right now—to make sure she feels secure, happy, content, but she doesn't need that right now. She just needs me...my touch.

I pull away, exhaling a ragged breath. Keira's chest heaves, pressing her breasts up with each breath. As I stare down at my soon-to-be wife, her beauty reflecting upon me, my brother's words pop into my head.

"Damon, I need you to come to the mansion. We have some important matters to discuss, and you should bring Keira as well."

I'm not dumb enough to think this was a coincidence. The fact that my brother called and demanded I come to his home, then Hayley has a mental breakdown and shows up at my house with a gun—it's all fishy as fuck, and I'm going to figure out what the hell is going on.

"Baby, we need to go pack a couple bags. We're going to go stay with Xander for a little bit." Worry flickers in her eyes, and I know she's still in shock. She's going to need some time to digest all this.

"Actually, you know what, wait here, I'll pack some stuff."

"Okay," she mumbles, not even making a move to get up.

I rush upstairs to our bedroom, my feet slamming against the wood floor with each step. When I make it to the room, I go through the drawers, grabbing panties, bras, T-shirts, yoga pants —anything I can get my hands on. I pull a small suitcase from the closet and shove all the shit into it. I don't worry about my own clothing. I have a bunch of shit at Xander's place anyway. Once done, I race around the bathroom grabbing a bunch more of Keira's shit, and when I get back to the kitchen, I toss the suit-case aside and look at Keira. Her ass is still seated on the counter like she's a part of it.

"Are...?" I start, but the sound of the doorbell ringing interrupts us once again, and I grind my teeth together, pulling away.

"Stay put until they get the body out of here. Okay?" I hate the way I sound and how bossy I am being. I don't think she would get up anyway, since she hasn't moved since I put her on the damn counter.

Keira nods her head, placing her hands in her lap. She still seems shaken up, but I know she'll move on. She knows nothing's going to happen to me, and anyone who tries to hurt her may as well commit suicide because they're dead for trying.

I step over Hayley's body and peek through the glass, checking to make sure it's Toni. When I see his round face and two of my men flanking him, I open the door. After he and the other men enter, Toni's eyes scan the scene. He doesn't ask questions, and even if he did, I wouldn't give him answers. He doesn't need to know what happened. I pay him to clean up the mess and keep his mouth shut.

"Boss," the three greet me in unison, and I tip my chin at them.

"Make it look like an accident. I don't care what kind." My stomach churns as I walk away, leaving Toni to clean up the mess.

I march back into the kitchen, walk over to Keira, and cup her cheeks. I rub my thumbs up and down them, breathing deeply.

"Everything is going to be fine, baby. Everything is going to be fine," I whisper, praying like hell my words aren't a lie.

If anything happens to Keira, I'll kill everyone.

Every. Single. Person.

eira

I STARE at my hands as we stand in the kitchen, waiting for them to move Hayley's body. Her death hasn't fully sunk in. Strangely, I don't feel bad. You're supposed to feel bad when someone dies, right? I was sad when my brother died. I should be sad Hayley's dead. I should be terrified the man I love killed her, snapping her neck right in front of me.

He did it without thought—like his body knew what it was doing—like it was something he did every single day.

I'm still waiting for feelings to come, but I feel nothing. My emotions twist out of control, and all I can think about is I could've lost Damon—and if I had, it would've been at her hands.

A horrible thought enters my mind. I want to forget it, but once it's there, I can't seem to get it out. If I would have had the chance, I would have killed her myself. If I were as strong as Damon—no, I know I would have broken her neck myself.

Damon is standing right in front of me, watching me as if I'm seconds away from exploding. He's probably wondering how I'm going to handle all this. What would he think of me if he knew what I was conjuring up right now?

My dark thoughts are interrupted when Toni steps into the room.

"All done, boss."

"All right. Come on, baby." Damon offers me a hand, helping me off the counter. He guides me out of the room, grabbing the suitcase he packed on the way out.

We walk through the foyer where Hayley's dead body was laying across the floor. It's gone now, but my eyes are still fixated to the spot. I walk around the area like it's going to burn my shoes if I touch it—like the wood is tainted or something...as if her death has left an evil residue on the floor.

Damon holds my hand, practically dragging me out the door to his car like nothing happened. It's strange to go from someone dying to pretending like nothing happened.

When we make it to the car, he opens the door and all but lifts me into the passenger seat. I know I need to say something, anything, to make him aware I'm okay, but I don't want to say a word. I don't think I can without breaking down.

All I can think about is a world without Damon. I knew he was dangerous, that he came with an X on his back, but I guess, in my eyes, he seemed invincible. But after tonight, I know he's not. He's just as close to death as the rest of us—maybe even closer considering what he does for a living.

I don't even realize Damon's in the car and we're driving down the road until I catch a pair of headlights coming at us.

"Would you please say something?" Damon's white knuckling the steering wheel, clearly upset by my silence, but I don't know what to say that I haven't already.

"I'm okay," I mumble. I can see the worry in his gaze, and I don't want him to be concerned about me, because it's not me I'm worried about. It's going to take time, but I'll be okay.

I spent so much time trying to run from him and fearing him, only to end up being terrified of losing him. Even after all this, all we've been through, all he's done, I love him beyond this life.

I'll love him forever.

For the rest of the drive, I stare out the window and watch the scenery whizzing by while I try to remember the person I was this morning. Damon doesn't say anything else after I tell him I'm okay, and I'm thankful.

We pull up to the Rossi mansion, and I take a deep breath before opening my door at the same time Damon does. We both get out of the car, and Damon grabs the suitcase from the back. My feet feel heavy as I trudge up the stairs, my hand in his. It isn't until we're halfway to the front door that I notice Xander standing at the top, waiting for us just like he did last time. He looks like the king. Like he owns the whole fucking world.

"Little brother, I wasn't expecting you today. I thought we agreed on tomorrow," Xander calls out in a cheerful voice. He gives me a smile, showing off his straight white teeth.

I blink, my gaze swinging to Damon's, wondering why Xander was expecting us tomorrow. I know right away there's something he isn't telling me, and I don't like it. Not at all. Damon gives his brother a heated glare, looking as if he's about to break someone's neck again.

"Let's get inside and have a drink before we talk about anything." Damon sounds irritated, and his tone confirms my hunch that there is something going on I don't know about.

"Be my guest." Xander gestures for us to enter.

Damon's hand tightens in mine, and he pulls me over the threshold and into the house.

Did I mention I hate being here?

We walk into the dining room, and my eyes move to the table where we had dinner, then out over the patio and garden.

"We should really discuss this in my office." Xander's eyes bore into mine. "Alone."

I want to smack the stupid right out of him. If he thinks I'm giving them privacy than he's dumber than I thought.

"She goes with me. Someone just fucking shot at her, and I had to kill the bitch, so I don't really care what you have to say about it, Xander."

"Fine. I see you are in a foul mood. Maybe you should just call it a night and we'll talk tomorrow when you are more...settled." Xander gives us a wicked smile and steps aside for us to pass.

"You're right. Let's go get some rest. We'll deal with this tomorrow." Damon tugs me past Xander and up the staircase. I don't complain. Lying down in a bed right now sounds amazing—especially when Damon is going to be lying next to me.

I practically sprint up the stairs. I'm more than eager to get away from Xander, ready to lock myself in the bedroom with Damon. As soon as we enter, the lights filter on and he closes the door, flicking the lock into place. I highly doubt that lock would stop his brother from coming in, but I guess it's the thought that counts.

"I'm sorry." Remorse, maybe even guilt, coats Damon's words. It doesn't sound right—the word "sorry" falling from his lips. I get the feeling he doesn't say it often...if at all.

"Why? You don't have anything to be sorry for," I say, turning around to face him once my ass hits the bed. He releases the suitcase, and it falls to the floor with a thud. Then he's on me, crossing the space between us in a second.

"I'm sorry because I brought you into this shit world. You could've left—hell, you should've, but you stayed. And after tonight, after how close I came to losing you...it's killing me I might have lost you."

"Damon, you didn't bring me into this, my brother did." The words pain me, but that doesn't make them any less true. I know Leo was trying to support me, and that makes my guilt even worse, but in the end, it was Leo who got caught up in this. He could have found another way. We could have found another way together.

"My brother is the one who started this with whatever he did or didn't do for Xander. He got himself killed and left me to deal with his mess. You took me in when you didn't have to—you take care of me and protect me. So don't tell me sorry for doing what you do, when I wouldn't have it any other way."

There is so much more I want to tell him, but it doesn't seem like there are enough minutes in the day. I want to profess all the emotions coursing through me right now to him. I want to make sure he does not have an inkling of doubt in his mind about us. I want to tell him I'd kill for him too, and I couldn't imagine my world without him now. Damon is no longer just my protector. He's my soon-to-be husband—my everything. I want to tell him all that and more, but I can't, because his lips are pressed to mine in an all-consuming kiss.

I feel every single emotion in that kiss—adoration, lust, desire, safety. I feel it all. His tongue pushes into my mouth, and all I can think of is his tongue all over my body—on my neck, my breasts, my stomach, trailing all the way down to my pussy. My muscles clench around nothing but air, and I wish it was his tongue dipping inside me.

I moan into his mouth and grab onto his shirt. I fist the material in my hands, desperately wanting it off. He breaks the kiss long enough to give me a panty-melting smile before ripping my shirt off.

I hear material rip, but I don't care. Everything separating our bodies from becoming one is an inconvenience.

Slamming his lips back onto mine, our teeth clash. My arms snake around his neck, pulling him closer.

I need him closer...so much closer.

I feel his fingers unfasten my bra, and I help him get it off. With a gentle nudge backward, I'm lying on the bed as he peels off my yoga pants, then tosses the remnants to the floor.

I watch him start to take off his own pants, biting my lip when his huge cock finally springs free.

My body is restless. My thighs keep rubbing together in anticipation, and I can feel how wet I already am...just from kissing. I want more of him—his fingers, his mouth, his cock. I want him to own me and worship me—all at the same time.

"I want you, Damon," I purr, reaching for him.

I barely recognize my voice as my own, it's so heavy with need.

Damon lets out what sounds like a primal growl before he's back on me, his eyes as black as the night sky.

I spread my legs as wide as I can to give him full access, and he takes advantage. My body feels like molten lava, his gaze burning through me. Need floods me as I watch him fist his swollen cock, rubbing the tip all along my wet slit. My pussy clenches, begging with each flutter for more—for him.

"I want you, Damon. I want you to fuck me like you did last time we were here." I lift my gaze to his and cup his cheeks. I see confliction in his gaze.

"I...I don't know if I can." His voice cracks, and the way he's looking at me kills me. But I want him to know I trust him, that I love him. And I want him to know he'll never hurt me.

"You won't hurt me." I stretch to kiss him again, molding my lips to his. "I trust you, Damon. I love you, and I know you won't do anything to hurt me."

"I hurt you last time. I can't do that again. I vowed I wouldn't, and I won't."

His fingers trail down my arms, and I shiver at his touch, excitement zinging through my veins.

"Only in the beginning, and only because I wasn't ready. Trust me, I'm ready now, and I want you. I want you so bad it hurts." I lick my lips.

"Fuck, Keira." I watch him swallow. His gaze turns heated, and I can tell the moment he chooses to let go. There's a newfound roughness in his touch, and it's exhilarating.

"If you change your mind, just say the word," he murmurs against my lips before slanting his mouth against mine. The kiss is all-consuming, stealing air from my lungs. When his fingers dig into my hair, tilting my head back, I think I might explode.

He doesn't stick to kissing my lips—no, his mouth trails down my neck and over my chest, sucking on the tender flesh over my pulse. I fist the sheets as pleasure fills my veins.

I'm ready to melt when he suddenly pulls back, then stands next to the bed. I miss his skin on mine and whimper at the loss. Grabbing me under my knees, he pulls me toward him so my ass is hanging right at the edge of the bed.

His huge hands maintain their grip on my knees, and I can feel the silky, smooth head of his cock at my entrance. The contact makes my back arch off the bed. I'm ready...so ready for him. My pussy drips with need.

Peering down at me, his dark orbs remain on mine as he spears me with his cock. Air fizzles from my lungs, and my eyes drift closed for a moment as I relish in the slight burn of pleasure.

I cry out in bliss. There is no pain this time as his cock slides into my channel with ease. My eyes flicker open, but remain hooded as I watch him pull out and slam back in without pause.

His pupils are so dilated, I can't see any color. He's never looked so dangerous when touching me, and yet I don't feel any fear at all...only desire.

My hands reach for the sheets—for something that will help ground me to this bed.

He lets go of one of my knees and pushes it to the bed, spreading me wide. With his free hand, his fingers travel down my inner thigh to where we are joined, finding my center, and he puts the rough pad of his thumb on my swollen clit, all while never ceasing to thrust his rock-hard cock into me.

With him fucking me like this and his skilled fingers on my clit, it doesn't take me long to be panting and moaning like a wild cat in heat. My body thrashes, and I feel the orgasm coming.

Starting with a tingle low in my belly, the feeling spreads through my body like a wildfire. Every cell in my body is burning up, scorching away—only to be reborn in the next moment.

I'm pretty sure I scream his name, my mind lost in need and lust. Thinking has been replaced with the instinct to take and give pleasure.

My voice is still useless by the time Damon flips me, bending me over the edge of the bed. He doesn't waste any time, entering me again before I know what's happening, making me moan into the mattress.

"Is this what you wanted, wife? To be owned? To have my cock claim you?"

I'm a mess, and I can't even form a coherent response, so I just moan louder.

His hands roam over my ass and back, leaving goosebumps in their wake, and then out of nowhere, I feel a sting, the effects of his hand having slapped one of my ass cheeks. I slip forward and sigh as he massages the pain away.

"Mmmm, your pussy is impossibly wet. I can hear how much you want me." His hot breath touches my ears, the words sending me spiraling out of control. In this new position, he is hitting a different spot, a deeper one. This angle means I can feel his head hit the back of my channel, leaving his balls to slap my clit.

His hands settle on my hips—which he uses as leverage—pulling me toward him every time he thrusts. I can feel each stroke in my bones.

I don't know how long he fucks me like this. Could be minutes or hours, but I'm somewhere lost in oblivion where time doesn't exist.

Only pleasure and bliss. Only Damon Rossi.

When I feel another orgasm sneaking up on me, the sensation is so strong, I freak out for a split second, wondering if it might be too much. My pussy clenches so hard, it nearly hurts, and every muscle inside me tenses. My body goes rigid for a moment, then a warm wave of ecstasy washes over me.

I can feel Damon slow while I ride out every last aftershock.

"I love it when you milk my cock like that. When your pussy grips me so tight, my balls ache. And you're going to do it one more time for me."

I honestly don't know if I can. I'm already so wrung out. I don't know how Damon keeps this up. His stamina is insane.

His dick still feels hard—maybe even harder than when he started fucking me. My throat aches as I swallow, and my voice is hoarse from moaning and crying so much. All I can muster is a quiet whimper.

"I...I don't know if I can," I whimper, my body shaking, my heart racing out of my chest. I have a hard time getting the words out between Damon's steady thrusts—each one promising love and endless pleasure.

"Oh, you will, baby. You're gonna come so fucking hard around my cock. I want you to squeeze me, give me that orgasm, baby. Squeeze my cock. Milk every last drop of cum from me."

He doesn't sound like he is going to take no for an answer, and something about his demanding tone has me riding another wave of pleasure.

I feel a hand ghost against my ass cheeks, squeezing and kneading the flesh. Without warning, he reaches around and drags his fingers over my sensitive clit, past where we're joined.

"You're so fucking wet. Your juices are dripping down your leg."

Normally, that would be embarrassing, but it's not. It's hot as hell.

I whimper, wishing he would rub my clit again, but he doesn't.

Instead, he slips his fingers between my ass cheeks. I gasp when he finds my puckered asshole and starts to massage it.

My back stiffens, and Damon moves his other hand from my hip and pushes me down, forcing me deeper into the mattress.

I feel the panic start, my body clamming up.

"Keira, I'm not going to hurt you. I promise this is going to be nothing but pleasurable for you." His voice is so reassuring, I sink back into the mattress. "Just relax. You're going to like this. You're going to come so fucking hard, baby."

I want to tell him okay, but I am too far gone. I'm long past speaking. I do what he says and relax, letting him do whatever he wants to my body.

He continues massaging my forbidden hole, synchronizing it with his thrusts. Within a few strokes, I'm whimpering, feeling my orgasm build deep in my belly. I start to appreciate the foreign feeling of his finger on my asshole, and when my pussy starts to quiver, he slips one of his thick digits inside my ass.

Fear and excitement tingle through me as he continues to thrust deep inside my pussy while keeping his finger inside my ass. There is something so wrong...so dirty about this. It gives it an edge I can't really explain.

Suddenly, I want more. I want him to keep pushing, keep violating me. I shove my ass back into his finger, letting him know I want more.

"I told you would like this," he chuckles.

"Mmmhhh," is all I manage to get out, and the sounds are muffled by the mattress. My body shakes as he starts to move his finger in and out, slow at first, and faster as he pumps his cock deeper and deeper.

"You're sure a dirty girl. You're my dirty girl."

"Yes! Yes!" I scream, finding my voice.

"Come for me, beautiful. Come all over this cock. Show me who owns this cock."

His dirty words are all I need, and I fly, soaring over the edge. His finger slips from my ass, and he continues his thrust.

"I'm c-comminnggggg..." I cry. Blinding light appears before my eyes as I squeeze them shut.

As my pussy squeezes the life out of Damon's cock, he pounds into me harder. His grunts fill the air, and his thrusts are so deep, I think he might kill me.

"Fuck, baby...your pussy," he hisses through his teeth, and in seconds, I feel his warm seed fill my womb.

He holds onto me tightly, thrusting a few more times before pulling out all the way. When he does, I sag against the mattress, unable to do much of anything but breathe. His body lands beside mine, and he tucks me into his sweaty chest as if he too feels like he needs to be touching me all the time.

My eyes drift closed as I feel the thud of his heartbeat beneath my hands.

"I love you, Keira. I love you so much. I'm positive I loved you even before I met you."

I sigh. "Thank you for protecting me...for saving me," I murmur against his chest. "Thank you for letting me love you." My eyes grow heavier with each breath, and I know I'll never be safer than I am right now in Damon's loving arms.

22

amon

SHE FELL in love with a criminal...a fucking criminal—a man who didn't deserve her love. A man who was certain he was unable to love in return. She took him and shaped him into a man worthy of love. She didn't know what she had done or how much she had changed him, but every time he looked at her, he knew he wanted to be good—if only for her.

Thoughts swirl around my head, making it hard to sleep. Maybe a little midnight snack will help ease the insomnia. Gazing down at Keira, I feel I don't want to leave her, but I'm not waking her up to bring her downstairs with me.

She needs her sleep; she barely gets enough as it is. I peel her naked body from mine. She's sticky with sex, and I love that my scent clings to her skin, marking her as mine. I pull the comforter to her shoulders and slip from the bed, pulling on a pair of sweatpants.

I tiptoe from the room and close the door. Hopefully, she doesn't wake up while I'm gone. Being away from her even for a short time enrages me. I want her with me everywhere I go—to be my shadow. But even possessive-as-hell Damon realizes how fucked up that is.

The hall is dark, but I know this house like the back of my hand, and this monster isn't scared of anything. I walk down the hallway and hear a soft cry. It pierces the air, meeting my ears instantly.

I turn my head, pointing it in the direction I think I heard the cry. It's so strange. It sounds exactly like the noise I heard the last time I was here.

I hold my breath, so there is absolute silence surrounding me, and for a few moments there is. Then I think I must be going crazy for the second fucking time when it goes away, but a few seconds later, I hear it again.

My feet move to follow the sound when I hear something else. I stop again and strain my ears.

Is that Xander's voice?

I shake my head. There is no w—

Another low cry echoes through the hall, interrupting my thoughts, accompanied by Xander's soft voice. My brother's tone sounds soothing and kind, warm even. There's no fucking way that's my brother, but it's definitely his voice. I know it.

What the fuck?

I move farther down the hall and closer to the door where I'm pretty sure the crying is coming from. My stomach does a summersault the moment my hand grips the knob. I hear Xander's voice clearly now, and I'm more confused than I've ever been in my entire life.

The crying has stopped, replaced by the soft cooing of a baby.

This must be some sick joke. Some twisted fucking mind game of his. There is no way I'm going to believe my brother is caring for a baby...or has one.

I push the door open, whole-heartedly expecting him to be holding a tape recorder. What I see is biggest mindfuck of all.

A nursery decorated in light blue. A large, white crib. And Xander sitting in a rocking chair, holding a baby.

A. Fucking. Baby.

I can't take my eyes off the baby he's cradling in his arms. What the fuck is going on? Did he steal someone's kid?

"Come on in, little brother. It's time for you to meet your nephew."

I think I've lost the ability to blink—hell, to even speak or walk for that matter. This has got to be a nightmare.

I watch the small baby in Xander's arms reach up and wrap his tiny fingers around Xander's thumb.

"Don't just stand there, come look at him. He has a strong grip all ready. He'll be big and strong in no time." It's Xander's voice I'm hearing, but I'm unfamiliar with the tone. And the words don't make sense.

Once my legs start working again, I step all the way into the room and move to where Xander is sitting. I look down at the small child. He has big brown eyes and black hair—just like Xander.

"Have you ever held a baby?"

Xander doesn't wait for my answer. We both know what it is. Who the fuck would let *me* hold their baby?

Apparently, Xander. Because in the next moment, he gets up and places the baby in my arms.

I instinctively cradle it to my body, still not sure this isn't some fucked up joke.

"Where did you get this thing?" I question, staring down at the little boy who looks like a replica of my brother.

Xander chuckles. "I'm sure I don't need to explain how babies are made, and don't call my son a *thing* again. His name is Quinton."

I blink. "Okay, but seriously, where did you get him? We both know you will never claim a woman, and last I knew, you need a woman to give birth—not a man."

There is no amusement on his face. In fact, he looks pissed.

"Loving a woman is a weakness I cannot afford." He moves his gaze down to the baby still cradled in my arms. "And yes, a woman gave birth to my son...obviously, but she is out of the picture now." Xander takes him from my arms and places him into the crib.

He wraps him in a blanket and winds up the contraption hanging from the side of the railing. It starts to play a soft lullaby. It's such a mundane thing to do, and yet, watching my brother do it is anything but.

It's so strange. I've seen him kill in cold blood. I've witnessed his hands crushing a man's throat, and now, those same hands are cradling a baby.

"You killed her, didn't you?" my voice booms over the sound of the music. Of course I know the answer already, but Xander's evil smirk confirms it.

"Loyalty means everything to me. I discovered she was hiding things, exploiting information, so I did what I do with loose ends."

I roll my eyes. "You ended the life of your child's mother? How do you think he is going to feel about it when he's grown and finds out?"

I consider what I feel like when Keira becomes pregnant some-day. I could never picture killing her after she gave birth. The thought of killing her for any reason has my stomach twisting in pain.

"Don't look at me like that," Xander sneers. "She used me. She got herself pregnant, and then after she had our son, she tried to run away with him. Like I would ever allow that."

That's the thing about my brother. He offers zero chances. He's ruthless. For a long time, I didn't even think he had a heart—until I watched him cradle his baby boy to his chest.

I run a hand through my hair. I can't stop looking at the crib. It's impossibly hard to rationalize my criminally insane brother has a kid, and that he's raising it on his own. How the hell can he be a good dad when our dad wasn't?

J.L. BECK C. HALLMAN

"How is Keira?" The lazy smile on his lips bothers me.

"Fine. Shaken up, but she was more concerned with my well-being than her own. The bullet was meant for her."

"I told you to come here as soon as you could, but like always, you disagreed." Xander shakes his head, walking out of the room, a frustrated scowl on his face.

I follow him out. "What do you mean you told me? You knew about this, didn't you?" I'm livid. My blood pressure spikes. Of course he knew.

He doesn't answer, and he doesn't stop walking until we reach the study. I'm clenching my fists so hard, the muscles in my forearm ache.

"Answer me, Xander! Did you know? Because if you knew and something would've happened to Keira..."

"You'd what?" He lifts a brow, a glass of whiskey in his hands. "Shoot me? Kill me? What would you do to your big brother to protect the woman you love?"

Love...

"You don't know shit..." Fear for Keira's safety trickles up and down my spine.

Amusement twinkles in my brother's dark gaze. "Admit it. You love her. That's why you didn't hesitate to marry her. It's okay to admit you have a weakness."

My jaw aches as I start to grind my molars. "She's not a fucking weakness."

"But she is, isn't she?"

Is Keira a weakness? Maybe. But she can hold her own. It's my job—as her man—to be concerned for her safety, though. That's what a good man does.

"You judge me like you have no weakness of your own, but I must ask you, who's going to protect your son from all your enemies?"

Xander's facial features turn murderous. "My son is not a weakness—not if no one knows he exists."

I almost burst into a fit of laughter. "You're going to hide your son from the world because of a few enemies."

He brings the amber liquid to his lips, but doesn't drink. "We're past having a *few* enemies, little brother. Maybe when you were an active member of the family, we had a few, but I've done some things...changed things—and that's put more fire on us than we previously had."

"Okay, and hiding your son from the world forever is going to do what?"

"I'm not hiding him from the world. I'm hiding him until it's safe —or until he can protect himself."

Clearly, I'm not understanding this. "You're aware of who you are and what you do for a living, right?"

Xander's gaze turns cold. "I am. Are you? Because you continue to talk down to me like I'm scum beneath your shoe. I saved your whore upstairs from death, and I brought you back into the family. I've welcomed you with open arms, little brother, and all you've done is shit on me."

"Call Keira a whore one more time and I will slit your fucking throat." I know I'm feeding right into his hand—right into his sick game—but I won't let him talk about Keira like that...not when she isn't here to defend herself.

"This seems like very irrational behavior for someone who *isn't* in love." He has a dark smile plastered across his face.

His mood swings give me whiplash, and I want to punch him in the face a thousand times over.

"It doesn't matter, Xander. If I love Keira, then I do...so fucking what. Love isn't a weakness, and the sooner you learn that, the better your life will be."

He chuckles, then takes a huge gulp of his drink.

"You know what, brother," I sneer. "There is no hope for you. You're heartless and as sick as our father."

My words seem to cause him to snap. An eruption of violence breaks free, and within seconds, he's tossing the glass against the wall behind me. It shatters, and the remaining contents drip down the wall, but I don't flinch. My brother doesn't scare me. The only thing he could possibly hurt is upstairs, and I'd kill him if he ever laid a hand on her again.

"I'm nothing like our father. Nothing," he booms. "In fact, I've done every single fucking thing I could to make certain I didn't turn into that bastard, but since you're so keen on assuming I am just like him, why don't you fight this fucking war against him on your own?"

My brow furrows, confusion settling in. "What are you talking about? He's been dead for years. I watched you shoot him right after he shot me. He's dead."

A darkness falls over Xander's face. "No, we thought he was dead, but I can assure you he's not. And now that we both have a weakness worth fighting for, we need to protect the Rossi empire. We need to protect what's ours."

I can't believe my fucking ears. "You're telling me our father isn't dead?"

Xander stares me straight in the eye. "I'm telling you our father isn't dead, and he's coming for us next."

The ground beneath my feet seems to disappear, and I realize how bad this is going to get.

War. A full-out war is going to take place. Xander and I won once, but can we beat death again?

Can we beat the monster without becoming one ourselves?

Thank You for reading Protect Me.
Damon and Keira's story might be over, but Xander's book is just starting. If you loved Protect Me make sure you pick up a copy of **Keep Me.**

ALSO BY THE AUTHORS

***

DARK ROMANCE

The Blackthorn Elite
Hating You
Breaking You
Hurting You
Regretting You

The Obsession Duet
Cruel Obsession
Deadly Obsession

The Rossi Crime Family
Protect Me
Keep Me
Guard Me
Tame Me
Remember Me

The Moretti Crime Family
Savage Beginnings
Violent Beginnings
Broken Beginnings

The King Crime Family
Indebted
Inevitable

ABOUT THE AUTHORS

J.L. Beck and C. Hallman are an USA Today and international bestselling author duo who write contemporary and dark romance.

For a list of all of our books, updates and freebies visit our website.

www.bleedingheartromance.com